THE BHAGAVADGĪTĀ

THE BHAGAVADGĪTĀ

translated from the Sanskrit by

Professor Vrinda Nabar *&*
Professor Shanta Tumkur

WORDSWORTH CLASSICS

For customers interested in other titles from Wordsworth Editions

Visit our web-site at
www.wordsworth-editions.com

Or for our latest list and a full mail order service contact:

Bibliophile Books
5 Thomas Road
London
E14 7BN

Tel: (0044) 020 7515 9222
Fax: (0044) 020 7538 4115
e-mail: orders@bibliophilebooks.com

This edition published 1997 by Wordsworth Editions Limited
8b East Street, Ware, Hertfordshire SG12 9HJ

ISBN 1 85326 197 1

1 3 5 7 9 10 8 6 4 2

Typeset by Antony Gray
Printed and bound in Great Britain by
Mackays of Chatham plc, Chatham, Kent

CONTENTS

PREFACE

Several translations and commentaries on the *Bhagavadgītā* exist, many of them comprehensive and thorough. In my Bibliography, I have indicated some of those which any reader whose interest is aroused may well want to look at. I have tried to make this edition different, not at the expense of the text's metaphysical framework, but by placing that framework in the present-day context. The questions raised in the Introduction are ones which also perplex many Hindus. They could therefore be seen as part of a common global think-tank in which all students of the *Gītā* may want to participate.

Many Hindus (Brahmins and non-Brahmins) are agnostics, and the divinity of the *Bhagavadgītā* has little significance for them. At the same time, its placement in the *Mahābhārata* and the part played by Kṛṣṇa in the epic and in the *Gītā* have their own independent appeal. The Introduction attempts to view these in perspective while in no way falsifying the traditional framework of Hindu thought within which the text is located.

The translation is, hopefully, 'imaginatively thorough' – while adhering to the letter, it endeavours, as far as possible, to iron out the clumsinesses in syntax arising from transferring a highly elaborate ancient rhetoric to the pragmatic framework of English syntax. I have however resisted the temptation to 'Englishise' it *in toto*, because it would then not be the *Bhagavadgītā* at all. I am grateful to my collaborator in translation, Professor Shanta Tumkur, for her patience and cooperation.

Others who deserve mention are Professor Sindhu Dange of the Sanskrit Department at Bombay University, my brother-in-law Suren Navlakha for his help in locating much useful material, and my husband Sumit Bhaduri for once again being a willing whetstone for my intellectual energies. Finally, many thanks to Tom Griffith who started me off on this enormously satisfying project and who was always accessible and sympathetic to the problems involved.

VRINDA NABAR

INTRODUCTION

THE BHAGAVADGĪTĀ IN INDIAN LIFE

The first thing about the *Bhagavadgītā* that any non-Hindu or non-Indian needs to understand is that it incorporates what may broadly be termed the Hindu view of life more than any other extant Hindu text. Though almost 2,500 years old, it is very much a part of Indian thought and world-outlook. The symbolic importance the *Bhagavadgītā* holds for the average Indian indicates the extent to which, for most Indians, time present is contained in time past.

It is impossible to ignore the *Bhagavadgītā* in India. Newspapers contain extracts from it almost every day, just as politicians and public speakers draw upon its innumerable *ślokas* to illustrate their stand. It even forms part of advertising copy. The important thing about this large-scale pervasiveness is that the *Bhagavadgītā* does not feature merely as a convenient, extraneous source for quotations. It constitutes a substantial part of the actual sub-structure of present-day thought for most Indians (or at least for the Hindus who form the single largest social group). Ultimately, one returns to it, either in acceptance or rejection.

At the same time, paradoxically, the presence of the *Bhagavadgītā* does not appear to have made any significant difference to the direction in which Indian society has moved. Its tacit acceptance, though not 'hypocritical', is embedded in a fundamental contradiction between ideology (or faith/belief) and social practice. All its exhortations of detachment from the fruits of action, its insistence on the importance of action as an end in itself, have not stopped Indian society from its obsessive quest for the material, perceived as the only index of individual and social success.

It is wrong to assume therefore, as so many Westerners do, that the spiritual message of the *Upaniṣads* or the *Bhagavadgītā* offers an alternative direction of social growth which is reflected in contemporary Indian society. On the contrary, present-day Indian social aspirations are, most of them, shaped by the late twentieth-century market-driven world-view of the West. This is no doubt an inevitable consequence of the global-village syndrome, and at one level becomes necessary for one's very survival. However, the continued acceptance of the *Bhagavadgītā* as spiritual text on the Indian scene indicates that there are indeed more things under our heaven and earth than could be dreamed of in a contemporary Western perspective.

Though interpretations of the *Bhagavadgītā* are numerous and, by and large, thorough, it is doubtful whether most Indians would be conversant with these. For them, its *raison d'être* is to be found in the epic called the *Mahābhārata*. It should be pointed out here that the *Mahābhārata* and the *Rāmāyana* are not epics in the sense that one understands the term with reference to, say, the *Iliad* or the *Aeneid*: texts that have at best socio-cultural and literary value. They are seminal to Indian life even today, and have an overwhelming relevance to contemporary Indian thought. Of the two epics, again, while the *Rāmāyana* for a variety of reasons may have a more sentimental appeal to Indians, it is the *Mahābhārata* which is undoubtedly richer and more complex in range. It encompasses philosophy, heroic values, political theory, ethics and norms of conduct. It is enormously elastic in its capacity to incorporate other themes, such as the caste-structure or the contextual parameters by which actions are to be judged, presented through parables and fables which have an ultimate bearing on moral truths.

THE MAHĀBHĀRATA

The *Mahābhārata* contains about 100,000 couplets, and is the story of the descendants of the Kuru dynasty. What concerns us here is that it describes the fortunes of two brothers, Pāṇḍu and Dhṛtarāṣṭra, sons of the King of Hastināpur. Pāṇḍu became the ruler of Hastināpur when his father died, as his brother, though older, was blind. An unfortunate accident resulted in Pāṇḍu's exile and ultimate death, and placed Dhṛtarāṣṭra on the throne. The five sons of Pāṇḍu and his widowed wife Kuntī returned to Hastināpur after his death, and were under the protection of Dhṛtarāṣṭra. Of the five sons, Yudhiṣṭir was the oldest and represented truth and virtue. Bhīma, the second, was the strong one, while the third brother, Arjuna, was one of the most famed among archers. Dhṛtarāṣṭra had a hundred sons by his wife Gāndhāri, and the oldest among them was Duryodhana.

In the Introduction to his rendering of the *Bhagavadgītā*, Juan

Mascaro describes Duryodhana as the incarnation of evil (the *Bhagavad-gītā*, Penguin India, 1994, p.21). This is a somewhat simplistic evaluation of Duryodhana, whose basic failing was a form of ambition and arrogance fuelled by an overwhelmingly fatalistic world-view. It was easy for his mother's disgruntled brother Sakuni to manipulate Duryodhana's weakness and lack of self-control. At the same time, Duryodhana had redeeming features. He was the only one who befriended Karṇa (Kuntī's unacknowledged son, born out of wedlock and brought up by a charioteer), ignoring the fact that he was apparently low-born at a time when caste played a significant part in social operations. While it may be argued that Duryodhana was motivated by self-interest (he hoped to use Karṇa in his fight against the sons of Pāndu), it has to be admitted that he was always a good friend to him.

During one of their several exiles, the Pāṇḍavas heard of the *swayaṁvar* of Draupadī, daughter of King Drupad. The *swayaṁvar*, at which Draupadī would garland the suitor who proved worthy of her hand, attracted kings and princes from all over India. To show he was eligible, the suitor had to shoot with an arrow the eye of a revolving fish that was placed at a height. He had to do this, moreover, by looking down at the reflection of the fish in water. The Pāṇḍavas went to Drupadī's court in the guise of Brahmins, and Arjuna was the man who eventually won Draupadī's hand.

Popular legend has it that the brothers returned to the forest with Draupadī, entered their hut to find Kuntī cooking their dinner, and jocularly asked Kuntī to see what the day's begging for alms had yielded (the Brahmin ascetic traditionally begged for his daily alms). Kuntī, who had her back to them, said what she always did: Share it among yourselves. This casual remark became binding on the five brothers who, 'sharing' Draupadī, became her five husbands.

This marriage of Draupadī to the Pāṇḍava brothers has intrigued many scholars of socio-anthropology who see it as a recorded account of the existence of polyandry. Some of them have even offered interesting theories about it being symbolic of the transition from the earlier, maternal, polyandry to the system of fraternal polyandry and, therefore, of the growing strength of patriarchy.

Duryodhana's overreaching ambition compelled his doting father to name him the Crown Prince even though Yudhiṣṭir had the rightful claim to be the next king. Though the Pāṇḍavas accepted all these injustices, the persistent machinations of Duryodhana and Śakuni left them with no option but to fight their cousins, the Kauravas. Among the various stages leading to this point of no return was the infamous game of dice to which the Kauravas challenged them, in which the 'virtuous' Yudhiṣṭir, having lost, staked everything he had, including, eventually, Draupadī. Humiliated in front of the assembly, it was she who ultimately won them all a royal reprieve.

However, after being defeated a second time at dice, the Pāṇḍavas had to spend twelve years in the jungle and a thirteenth one without their identity being detected. After the thirteen years were over, the Kauravas refused to return their kingdom to them, rejecting even their final demand for a mere five villages. It was at this point that the Pāṇḍavas challenged their cousins to open war. Their decision to do so was supported and even engineered by Lord Kṛṣṇa, who was not merely an *avatār* (incarnation) of the god Viṣṇu but also their maternal cousin. Kṛṣṇa and Arjuna had always been especially close, and when the Pāṇḍavas set out for war, Kṛṣṇa deliberately volunteered to be Arjuna's charioteer. His purpose in doing this becomes clear when one reads the *Mahābhārata*, and the more so in the context of the *Bhagavadgītā*. It is Kṛṣṇa who manipulates events so that the battle ends in the victory of the Pāṇḍavas, even though the actual choices and their execution through action are apparently left to them.

The battle between the Pāṇḍavas and the Kauravas, fought on the field of Kurukṣetra to the north of present-day Delhi, is supposed to have lasted eighteen days. It is worth noting that the *Mahābhārata* contains eighteen books or *parvans*, the *Bhagavadgītā* eighteen sections or *adhyāyas*.

It was when the two armies were drawn up for battle that Arjuna, looking across, felt paralysed and unable to fight. The real implications of this battle – that it would be a fight to the finish between different members of his own family – reduced him to confusion and anguish. Seeing men like his former guru Droṇācārya and his great-uncle Bhīṣma in the opposite army, Arjuna no longer knew whether the war was necessary or who deserved to win (Chapter 2, verse 6). It was at this point that Kṛṣṇa supposedly preached the *Bhagavadgītā* to him. The long poetic discourse is said to be named after Kṛṣṇa who was also known in the Bhāgavata faith as Bhagavān.

The *Bhagavadgītā* occupies Chapters 22 to 40 of the Bhīṣmaparvan of the *Mahābhārata* and each of its *adhyāyas* or chapters has a definite heading or theme. It is believed to have been originally composed by Vyāsa-munī, who is also credited with having authored the *Mahābhārata*. There is some controversy as to its exact date of composition, but it is generally agreed that it must have been composed some time around the fourth or fifth century BC.

Within the context of the *Mahābhārata*, and especially the battle of Kurukṣetra, the existence of the *Bhagavadgītā* clearly calls for a willing suspension of disbelief. There is no other way in which one can accept the fact that the two sides waited to begin the war while its eighteen *adhyāyas* were recited. Yet this detail seems superfluous when one is face to face with the philosophical and sociological significance of the *Bhagavadgītā*. Interpolation or otherwise, Hindus would by and large unquestioningly accept its presence in the *Mahābhārata*. In their eyes, the epic is enriched by its presence while it, in turn, draws its abiding appeal from its context.

A SUMMARY OF THE BHAGAVADGĪTĀ

The war in the *Mahābhārata* was fought on the field of Kurukṣetra which, in the very first line of the *Bhagavadgītā*, is also described as a *dharmakṣetra*, viz. a sacred field (*kṣetra* means field) or field of righteousness. Kurukṣetra was once an open field surrounding Hastināpur, said to be where present-day Delhi is located. According to popular myth Kuru, common ancestor of both the Kauravas and the Pāṇḍavas, ploughed this field with his own hands. The god Indra is supposed to have blessed Kuru by stating that anyone who died on that field either in war or while engaged in some form of religious austerity would attain Heaven. Hence the term *dharmakṣetra* came to be applied to it.

When the war between the Pāṇḍavas and the Kauravas was about to begin, Vyāsa supposedly offered Dhṛtarāṣṭra the gift of eyesight if he desired to see the war. Dhṛtarāṣṭra's reply was that he did not wish to be a witness to the annihilation of his clan. Vyāsa then gave Sañjaya (Dhṛtarāṣṭra's charioteer) the ability actually to see all that happened on the battlefield and describe it to Dhṛtarāṣṭra. At the first meeting, Sañjaya told Dhṛtarāṣṭra that the Kuru patriarch (Bhīṣma) had fallen. Dhṛtarāṣṭra was filled with grief, and wanted to hear every detail regarding the war. The *Bhagavadgītā* begins at that point where Sañjaya has just finished describing to Dhṛtarāṣṭra the arrangement of the armies on both sides. Dhṛtarāṣṭra's question to Sañjaya, the first verse of the *Bhagavadgītā*, leads Sañjaya to narrate the dialogue between Kṛṣṇa and Arjuna, which comprises the *Gītā*.

At the end of Chapter 1 Arjuna casts off his bow and arrow and sits down in the chariot, unwilling to fight this war and kill his kinsmen. His anguish continues at the start of Chapter 2, and prompts his mentor Kṛṣṇa to begin his discourse.

Kṛṣṇa places before Arjuna two options relating to the way one leads one's life: the Sāṁkhya way, which is that of Renunciation, and the path of Karma Yoga, or the performance of one's prescribed duty. While both bring Release, Karma Yoga is clearly seen as superior. No one has achieved liberation by giving up action (*karma*). If a man's reason is unwavering, and he is free from the desire for the fruit of action, he is liberated from the limiting aspects of actions performed while being attached to the objects of sense. Karma should be performed at least for the universal good, if not for oneself.

Chapters 2 to 7 develop arguments relating to the essence of Karma and its relationship to true Knowledge (Jñāna), Appearance (Māyā) and Reality (Brahman/Parameśvara). A liberated man, according to Kṛṣṇa, should engage in the practice of yoga and concentrate on becoming one with the Lord. For this, moderation in everything is essential. The Karma Yogin is placed above all others, whether ascetics, those who have knowledge, or those who mechanically perform action or ritual.

Chapters 8 to 10 extend these arguments and speculate about the nature and origin of time and the universe (it should be noted here that the Supreme One's day and night are believed to comprise a thousand *yugas* each. Since the four *yugas* in the human world, viz. Kṛta, Tretā, Dvāpara and Kali, are each made up of 4,320,000 years, this period, multiplied by a thousand, constitutes one day of Brahman!).

In Chapter 9, Kṛṣṇa says that those who worship Him with an end in view – even if that end is Heaven and its enjoyments – have to die and be born continually. But those who see Him as the end of their worship are transported by Him. He receives whatever is offered Him with devotion, however insignificant the offering. All who worship Him, even if they are of the sinful class – women, Vaiśyas (the traders, the third caste in the Hindu social hierarchy), Śūdras (the 'untouchables', the lowest caste) – obtain the highest state. That being so, the release of the Brahmin (the priestly caste, the highest in the Hindu hierarchy, with a virtual monopoly over education and the *Vedas*) or Kṣatriyas (the second caste, warriors by profession; kings and rulers also belonged to this caste) is not to be doubted – Arjuna should perform his task in the proper spirit and reach the Lord.

In Chapter 11, Arjuna is eager to see Kṛṣṇa's divine, imperishable form. Overwhelmed by the sight, he bows down to Kṛṣṇa. Kṛṣṇa tells Arjuna that even without him the death of all those gathered on the other side is certain, for He has killed them long ago – Arjuna is only a symbolic instrument of that act (a spectacular and striking statement about determinism!).

In Chapters 12, 13 and 14, the duality of appearance and reality is further dwelt upon and the concepts of *puruṣa* and *prakṛti* are introduced. Discerning readers of oriental philosophy may note the resemblance between 'Puruṣa' and 'Prakṛti' on the one hand and 'Yin' and 'Yang' on the other.

Chapters 14 to 18 deal with several themes that are derived from the concepts introduced earlier and/or give them a stronger foundation. Primary among these are the concepts of reincarnation (rebirth), Aum-Tat-Sat (I explain this term towards the end of the Introduction), Saṁnyāsa (Renunciation), and Tyāga (Abandonment).

Kṛṣṇa advises the performance of one's duties in accordance with one's prescribed *dharma* (*dharma* is often broadly interpreted as 'religion' but it should be understood that the scope of the term is much more elastic and incorporates a whole way of life). In the present context, *dharma* refers to the duties prescribed for each caste. Kṛṣṇa sees these as consonant with one's intrinsic nature, which is also viewed here as caste-based. Arjuna is exhorted yet again to give up his self-circumscribed view of action and surrender all action to the Lord. Kṛṣṇa's arguments succeed in converting Arjuna to a state of mind where he agrees to fight the war.

THE BHAGAVADGĪTĀ RE-EXAMINED

The *Bhagavadgītā* is far from being a monolithic text, conceived and composed at one go. It is generally accepted as being a later interpolation into the *Mahābhārata*. The presence in its argument of many different strands, some of them apparently contradictory or seeming to repeat an earlier position, is one more proof of the *Bhagavadgītā*'s multiple heritage.

If I were to sum up the various themes contained in the *Bhagavadgītā* I would see them as falling into three principal categories. The entire argument in the text leads up to one point, viz. that Arjuna would have to fight this war. The basic premise on which the whole discourse is founded therefore is his initial reluctance to do so. From this stage to the final one in Chapter 18, the argument encompasses the following:

1 Arjuna's having to come to terms with the death at his hands of his kinsmen whom he loves dearly. This is both an emotional and a moral dilemma;
2 A framework which attempts to answer fundamental questions relating to ethics, philosophical truths or doubts and metaphysical speculation;

3 The emphasis on *dharma* as a crucial factor controlling human destiny. Dharma in the Hindu world-view is a hold-all for nearly every kind of detail which pertains to living. Kṛṣṇa repeatedly refers to Arjuna's duties, defined not in an individualistic context but in terms of his *varṇa* (social class/caste). Dharma and karma are both seen as inextricably linked to varṇa.

To many Indians who may be ignorant of the scholarly debates surrounding the *Bhagavadgītā*, its most accessible *śloka*, and the one which seems best to encapsulate its message, is the one in the second *adhyāya* where Kṛṣṇa advises Arjuna to perform his karma without giving any thought to the fruits of his action. Kṛṣṇa's entire message is as follows: You have a right to the performance of action alone, its fruits are never within your control. Do not perform action with an eye to its fruits, *nor let there be in you any attachment to the non-performance of action*' (verse 47, italics added). In other words, while Kṛṣṇa exhorts Arjuna not to heed the rewards of action, He also cautions him against getting attached to inaction. It is important to remember this dual theme, for the second of these is frequently ignored and only the first perceived as the message of the *Gītā*.

In actual fact, while the first part of the message alone would seem to emphasise the importance of karma, this is even more emphatically stated in the second part, for it asserts the need for the individual to be perpetually immersed in performing his karma. Karma is therefore seen as an ongoing process, and it is the means by which one breaks through one's mortal constraints and merges with the Supreme Being.

Bal Gangadhar Tilak sees Karma Yoga as the essence of the message contained in the *Gītā*. Yet, as Tilak says, even mastering this yoga is not the end of the journey for living creatures. Mere acquisition of spiritual knowledge and superiority does not absolve one of the duty to act. Just as Kṛṣṇa, who transcends all mortal binds, is still engaged in the affairs of the world/universe, so the man of knowledge (i.e. the one who has obtained spiritual release) must continue to participate in his worldly commitments. As Sartre was to say about man's relationship with the world in a very different age and context, 'We do not survey the world, but rather are engaged' (i.e. committed).

Viewed in this perspective, Karma Yoga becomes one of the highest forms of human commitment, for it preaches disinterested action not for one's own benefit but for the action itself. It is obvious that every action would have its consequence, and it is implicitly hoped that whatever the immediate outcome of such action, the ultimate end will be one which is for the good of mankind. In this sense, it could even be argued that the doctrine of karma is among the most revolutionary of ideologies.

While this is essentially true, Karma Yoga has other, less desirable, implications. Karma Yoga means, above all, performing one's karma in the right spirit, i.e. without thought to its immediate, material benefits. Arjuna's karma for instance was that of a Kṣatriya. In the context of the war, it was the Kṣatriya's duty to fight the battle heroically which he had to perform. Yet, Arjuna had not chosen to become a warrior but was one by virtue of his varṇa. The unmistakable assumption in the argument therefore is that varṇa (which was inflexible and which to the modern mind may not necessarily be an acceptable parameter) decided one's karma. Moreover, it was hopeless to try and break out of the bind of varṇa.

The varṇa-dharma-karma nexus is emphasised by Kṛṣṇa even at the end of the *Bhagavadgītā*: 'O Vanquisher of foes, the duties of Brahmins, Kṣatriyas, Vaiśyas and Śūdras are distinctively prescribed in keeping with the qualities inherent in their natures . . . Action according to one's own dharma, though flawed, is better than another dharma, though easy to execute. In performing one's naturally ordained duty, a man does not incur sin' (Chapter 18, verses 41 and 47).

It is this emphasis on varṇa-based karma that D. D. Kosambi had in mind in maintaining that the *Gītā* was sung for the upper classes by the Brahmins, and only through them for others. Kosambi quotes from the *Gītā* the lines where Kṛṣṇa refers to all those who take refuge in Him, 'be they women, Vaiśyas, Śūdras and others born in a sinful class'. The term used to describe these categories is *pāpayoni*. It was not a term commonly used for any of them, and referred to those with criminal tendencies. Therefore, a possible rationale for Kṛṣṇa's statement here is that because the *Vedas* were traditionally forbidden to women, Vaiśyas and Śūdras, they could not easily obtain Release except through the path of Devotion. Yet one cannot today overlook the categorical assumption that the two lower varṇas, along with *all* women, constituted a 'sinful class'! The message of the *Gītā* therefore is not as unqualifiedly revolutionary as would appear. It makes no allowances for the kind of social mobility which has now become an accepted feature of Hindu society.

At the same time, the *Gītā* has clearly transcended these limitations of contextual constraint and survived as a fundamental repository of Hindu values. This could only be because it contains a basic ideology which is not unacceptable within a certain socio-cultural and philosophical tradition.

Embedded in the *Bhagavadgītā* are several assumptions about the nature of the universe and of those who inhabit it. These in turn revolve around the nature of the Creator of the universe, who is both above it and contained in every aspect of it. It is this essence that Kṛṣṇa keeps returning to again and again.

In the second *adhyāya*, Kṛṣṇa tells Arjuna of the eternity of the Spirit and of the transitory nature of the body and of sense-perceptions. By transferring Arjuna's purely human anguish to a metaphysical plane, Kṛṣṇa distinguishes between what is Real (in the *Bhagavadgītā* this begins to mean an existence beyond the purely material one of sensory perceptions) and the Unreal (an existence circumscribed by material considerations).

According to Kṛṣṇa, only true knowledge can make Arjuna perceive this, and he should try to acquire it by performing his dharma/duty as a Kṣatriya (i.e. through warfare). Emphasiszing that action, and not the fruit of action, should be one's goal, Kṛṣṇa says that the Reason of the man who acts (*kartā*) in this spirit is superior to the act (*karma*). Such a man is free from turmoil and from emotions like desire and anger, products of attachment to the objects of pleasure. He is in what may be described as the Brāhmic state, where his peace merges with that of his god.

This line of reasoning remains central to the argument in the *Gītā*, and necessitates the repeated assertion of the nature of the supreme deity. In this the *Gītā* would seem to follow the mode of the *Upaniṣads* which do not define through positive assertions of what is but through the negative aspect, viz. what is not. Thus, over and over again, we read that the supreme reality is not this, nor this (*na iti, na iti*). Similarly, in the *Gītā*, the aspect of the Supreme Deity 'not being' either this or that is repeatedly stated:

> the Supreme Brahman [is] without beginning, said to be neither imperishable nor perishable . . . He pervades everything, abiding in it. He gives the impression of having the qualities of all the senses, yet is without the senses. Though unattached, He still supports everything. Void of qualities, He enjoys them nevertheless. He is outside and within all things. He is immovable and yet movable . . . Far away, He is still near . . . [Chapter 13, verses 12–15]

The *Bhagavadgītā* embodies the Deism also present in the *Vedas* and the *Upaniṣads*. Yet its context, viz. the dialogue between Arjuna and Kṛṣṇa, personalises the presence of the Supreme while in no way minimising the Law that is at the heart of all His actions.

Dr S. Radhakrishnan's view is that of the three aspects of the Supreme (Brahma, Viṣṇu and Śiva) the *Gītā* represents that aspect which is at work saving the world, and redeeming it from chaos. Hence, according to him, the importance of Kṛṣṇa, an embodiment of Viṣṇu.

This aspect of redemption is certainly emphasised in the *Bhagavadgītā*. Early on (Chapter 4, verses 7–8), Kṛṣṇa tells Arjuna that He takes birth whenever unrighteousness takes precedence over righteousness. Elsewhere, Kṛṣṇa reasserts that He is there for all true seekers who abandon the path of unrighteousness and merge with His truth through the proper performance of karma.

The relation between Brahman or the Supreme and the world is clearly an unequal one. From this apparently one-sided relationship derive other aspects of human existence which are expounded at length in the *Gītā*. Primary among these is the concept of Māyā.

While the Supreme creates the shapes and forms of the world He is himself without shape or form, and can only be defined through negatives. He is within our framework of time, yet beyond it, outside it, in a span which can be termed the Eternal. While the Eternal is beyond time, time is located within that Eternal. Similarly, though not dependent on the world, the Supreme is involved in its activity. The world is born of the two forms of the Supreme, *puruṣa* (the divine essence) and *prakṛti* (matter), which is also part of Him, but is the baser aspect, the one He has to work on. Whereas the element of *prakṛti* has been overcome in the Supreme Himself, it still exists in the material world, often offering resistance to the force of *puruṣa*. This resistance is a symptom of its corrupted form, and only when this resistance is overcome can the world be truly united with the Supreme.

If the Supreme is true being, it follows that the world is non-being, at best on the way to becoming. More accurately, it represents the constant struggle between the two states – being and non-being moving towards becoming. This state in which the two are interlocked is the state of Māyā, and it represents the power of the Supreme working on the world of matter or the universe.

It is erroneous to suppose, as people popularly do, that Māyā signifies mere illusion. Rather, it creates a defective consciousness in which we perceive the material world as our reality. We thus lose sight of the only reality – God – and become obsessed with the sensual world of material enjoyment. It is this defect in consciousness which produces pain and unhappiness, for it distances man from the divine purpose. Kṛṣṇa warns Arjuna that only those who surrender to Him can swim through the waters of Māyā (Chapter 7, verses 13–14).

In the *Bhagavadgītā*, Māyā broadly indicates the power which the Supreme brings to bear on *prakṛti*. This power is in Him because He combines both – He is the Imperishable as well as that which perishes, Immortality as well as Mortality. He uses this power to create mortal nature, and unless men fail to perceive this Māyā they become besotted with this fallible *prakṛti*. It is essential for man to remember that since God is the cause, He is the reality which transcends all the conflicts in the world He has effected – conflicts which arise from the inadequacies of its material nature.

At a very basic level, therefore, the *Bhagavadgītā* seems to posit an evolutionary process by which the human creature progresses towards a state of being which is one with the Supreme purpose. This aspect of the divine *puruṣa* is there in man's inmost core, and it is for him to draw it out till it no longer remains concealed but forms his very consciousness. Merely giving in to the demands of our social role will not bring about this awakening: one would need to see these finally as emerging from a deeper spiritual impulse which performs social duties without becoming attached to the bonds of the world or the consequences of such performance.

It is possible for man to endeavour to transfigure *prakṛti* with the help of *puruṣa*, so that they are not in conflict but in the kind of equation that is more representative of the Supreme. Moreover, man is a free agent even though the future is contained in the Eternal vision of the Supreme. Though Kṛṣṇa advises Arjuna, the choice of what to do next is left to him. At the same time, the *Gītā* makes it clear that man must consistently act in the proper frame of mind in order to obtain release. Release is that point at which the freedom of choice becomes superfluous, because this proper frame of mind has become as natural to man as breathing.

To reach this stage, man has first to acquire the proper *buddhi* – perception and understanding – which makes him see the situation he faces in its proper perspective. The *Gītā* emphasises this and the ways in which this can be achieved, but the sequence and the ways suggested may seem confusing and repetitive to the uninitiated. Even Arjuna has to seek elucidation and clarification several times in the course of the eighteen *adhyāyas*. It is not easy to summarise the complexity of thought without reference to the traditions from which this thought springs, but the following may be of some initial use.

Kṛṣṇa's long discourse is not merely a theoretical/metaphysical exposition, but goes beyond that and is even prescriptive. Three distinct disciplines are indicated, but it is important to note that these are far from being mutually exclusive and are in many respects complementary to one another. The three disciplines are: Jñāna Yoga, Bhakti Yoga and Karma Yoga. We all have some idea of what the term yoga means – a kind of intense discipline which enables us to control, even strengthen our psychic potential.

Kṛṣṇa's discourse makes it clear that mere action is not sufficient to secure release, for action is often performed in a blind manner by those who see karma as an end in itself and seek the rewards of karma. This, the way of those who do the right deed for the wrong reasons, only perpetuates the snare of karma, for it dooms the human being to a perpetual cycle of birth and doing. Though *jñāna* means wisdom, it is spiritual wisdom which is emphasised, for it shows us the path of true karma, the kind that ultimately liberates because it takes us close to the Supreme.

By practising Jñāna Yoga, man comes to an understanding of his selfhood – that quality which he has within him which is independent of the material and physical bondage of the body, and which releases him from all desire, greed and anguish. In the second *adhyāya* of the *Gītā*, Kṛṣṇa mentions Sāṁkhya Yoga but it is clearly Karma Yoga which He sees as more important. Sāṁkhya Yoga saw the two aspects of *puruṣa* and *prakṛti* as separate. Man can obtain release from the attractions of *prakṛti* by seeing that he has in him the ability to overcome its three dimensions: *sattva* or lightness, *rajas* or movement and *tamas* or heaviness. As against this the message of the *Gītā* is that through proper Karma Yoga man can know that these three objects of the material world are inseparable from the Supreme, as much part of Him as *puruṣa* (Chapter 7, verse 12). Inasmuch as God Himself has created these three, they are part of His Māyā: only those who seek refuge in Him can circumvent this Māyā (Chapter 7, verse 14).

The conviction that salvation or release can only come through identification with God brings us to the discipline of Bhakti Yoga. The message of the *Gītā* is of a God deeply involved in the affairs of the universe. It advocates *bhakti*, or loving devotion to God, while warning of the folly of loving the wrong gods. Worshipping them does not bring doom but it does not bring release either: as long as man remains caught in the snares of false worship he will continue to be a prisoner to the bondage of karma. It is not mere action that ensures release, but a reaching out for God's love and grace. At the same time, mere surrender without action is not enough.

Kṛṣṇa emphasises man's role in the earning of grace when he says that the Lord is impartial to all human creatures (Chapter 9, verse 29).

Repeatedly He states that the true man of action, who acts without thought for reward and surrenders to God, will be released from the bonds of karma. Release is therefore viewed as something which is the result of the mutual love between God and man. Man's love makes him surrender his actions to God and perform them only through love of Him.

The man who acts in this manner is led to true wisdom. Thus Bhakti Yoga and Jñāna Yoga clearly work in tandem. Yet bhakti is meaningless in the absence of action. Karma Yoga therefore is inextricably linked to these two other yogas. Emphasising that Arjuna's doubts are the result of his ignorance, Kṛṣṇa advocates the performance of karma in a detached spirit in order to reach the Lord. Men who renounce the world in search of knowledge can also obtain release, but the worth of Karma Yoga is greater than that of Karma Sāṁkhya (Chapter 5, verse 2) because action without desire is itself a form of renunciation. Just as the Lord never ceases to be involved, so it should be with all those who wish to reach Him.

Karma Yoga also includes the performance of tasks that may be difficult for a variety of worldly reasons. Not all actions are pleasant, but they are often necessary because they uphold a system of values and ethics. Though the war which occasions the *Bhagavadgītā* is one which Arjuna would rather not fight because it involves the possible killing of those who are very dear to him, his karma is to go beyond his immediate sense of distaste and address his action to the principles that call for action at that moment. Unless one surrenders all action to the source from which it ultimately springs, one will not be free from the bonds of karma. To act in this spirit of dedication and love is to be a true *saṁnyāsin*.

In the same context, Kṛṣṇa also tells Arjuna that God has already acted in the matter: Arjuna is only the symbolic instrument. In a cosmic sense, if all action is dedicated to God in a spirit of detachment, it could be said that it is God who acts through His agent – Arjuna is the *nimittamātram* (Chapter 11, verses 33–4). Just as God is active without being involved, so should His devotee seek to act without passion or involvement with worldly considerations.

The three yogas are therefore complementary, necessary to one another and to the human condition as long as the world remains corrupt. The cycle of karma can only end when every human creature has acquired true perceptions of jñāna, bhakti and karma. That is why it is necessary for the liberated soul to continue being active in the world.

CONCLUSION

Though the *Bhagavadgītā* is located within a Hindu context, it shares its basic concerns with other religio-cultural traditions. What is generally considered as metaphysical speculation in analytical philosophy deals with certain basic questions: Determinism versus Free Will; Essence versus Existence; issues relating to Epistemology; issues concerning Ontology; and so on. The history of philosophy by and large shows that these questions and the extent to which they can be answered by metaphysical speculation haven't changed very much. The content of the *Bhagavadgītā* is a striking example of the way in which fundamental questions (what Wittgenstein referred to as 'the unutterable') persist in human thought through the ages (have been 'contained unutterably in what has been uttered').

From this emerge several other issues related to the ethical aspects of action. Ultimately, especially to certain Western critics, the *Bhagavadgītā* appears to advocate action only in relation to total surrender to God. Knowledge, action and devotion find their end in love of God, transcending all earthly considerations. While this is at one level common to all religious philosophies, it is easy for such critics to see the *Gītā* as condoning any action as long as its end is the love of God. It is necessary to remind oneself therefore that Kṛṣṇa, shrewd statesman though He be, nowhere condones the evil in the world or in man. Repeatedly, both in the *Mahābhārata* and in the *Bhagavadgītā*, Kṛṣṇa asserts his purpose: to establish the rule of dharma in the world.

Though ostensibly propagating the supremacy of Viṣṇu, the *Bhagavadgītā* has become a fundamental Hindu text which transcends sectarian faith. At the same time, the multiple authorship of the *Mahābhārata* and the *Bhagavadgītā* represent the practice of a tradition which is not only non-plagiaristic but which actually negates plagiarism. Such a practice in turn leads to the apparent contradictions in both texts, as for example in the several aspects of Kṛṣṇa which unaccounted interpolations emphasise: his divinity; his diplomatic chicanery; the attempts to place him above all other divinities (a probable conflict between the Vaiṣṇav and Śiva cults); the projection of him as being pro-Brahmin and pro-yajña; his questionable views as regards women. Accepting such a rationale does not exonerate the limitations in the *Gītā*'s argument, but it does give it a wider perspective.

POSTSCRIPT

Since a comprehensive glossary would be almost as vast and complex as the *Bhagavadgītā* itself, I have listed below some of the terms I consider significant in reading a translated version.

1 AŚVATTHA: The aśvattha (peepal tree) is also known as the Brahmavṛkṣa, the Samsaravṛkṣa, Brahmavana and Brahmāraṇya – terms which link it to the Brahman and to the material world. The idea is to illustrate that just as the sky-high tree springs from a small seed, so has the colossal, visible universe sprung from the one and imperceptible Parameśvara.

2 AUM-TAT-SAT: In Chapter 17, verse 23, Kṛṣṇa says that the Supreme One (Parabrahman) is defined in the Scriptures as Aum-Tat-Sat, and that the Brahmins, the *Vedas* and the Sacrifices were created from this definition. It is obviously difficult to understand how anything could be created by a definition, and commentators have suggested that the word 'this' refers to the Parabrahman. In the *Gītā* the first Brahmin (in the form of Brahmadeva), the gods and yajñas are listed as the first among created things. But the form of Parabrahman from which all these have been created is contained in the three words Aum-Tat-Sat, and therefore what Kṛṣṇa says here is that this canon is at the root of the entire universe.

It is believed that any shortcoming in the performance of a sacrifice may be corrected by uttering one of the three words Aum-Tat-Sat. The Brahman, in the shape of the consonant Aum is supposed to have been the only thing in existence at the start of the universe. Therefore, all action or ritual begin with that letter. Tat represents that which is beyond ordinary action and which is desireless, while Sat refers to pure actions performed in accordance with Scriptural directions, even if they are performed in the hope of reward.

3 BHĪṢMA: Bhīṣma was Dhṛtarāṣṭra's grandfather and the patriarch of the Kuru dynasty. He was the son of the goddess Ganga and had the power to choose the moment of his death. In the war, though pierced with arrows, he postpones dying till the sun is in a specific position. He awaits that moment, lying prostrate on the arrows which have pierced him. At the start of the war, Duryodhana asks his forces to protect Bhīṣma on all sides because he had vowed never to fight a eunuch or a woman. The Pāṇḍava army contained Śikhaṇḍi, a eunuch, who was eventually the immediate cause of Bhīṣma's death. After the great war is over, Bhīṣma remains the

Kuru mentor, advising Yudhiṣṭhira each day about the intricacies of kingship. This continues till he dies.

4 DHANAÑJAYA: Winner of Wealth. Arjuna had located the hidden wealth of evil kings and used it for the public good. Hence he is called Dhanañjaya.

5 GUḌĀKEŚA: Arjuna is called Guḍākeśa because he had total control over sleep and was able to choose where and for how long to sleep. A man who has such control over sleep should have control over everything, but the *Gītā* shows that even such a man could succumb to an overwhelming situation, as happens with Arjuna.

6 JAPA-YAJÑA: *Yajña* means sacrifice. The fire-sacrifice is generally considered as the primary among all yajñas. However, in the bhakti (devotion) framework, *japa-yajña* or sacrifice through silent meditation is considered more important than the *havir-yajña* (fire-sacrifice). Manu (one of the seminal law-givers) has even stated (2.87) that whatever else a Brahmin does or does not do, he can attain salvation through silent meditation alone. Since the *Bhagavadgītā* incorporates Bhakti-Yoga, it emphasises japa-yajña.

7 HṚṢĪKEŚA: Lord of the Mind and Senses, i.e. Kṛṣṇa.

8 JANĀRDANA: Lord Kṛṣṇa, so called because he is worshipped by the people (*jana*) to attain true prosperity and deliverance.

9 KṚṢṆA: Kṛṣ connotes existence, ṇa bliss. Kṛṣṇa is the Being who combines Existence, Knowledge and Bliss. His dark blue colour represents infinitude. He is also the one who saves His devotees from distress.

10 MADHUSŪDANA: Lord Kṛṣṇa, so called because he killed the demon Madhu and made the world a safer place for sages to conduct their penance.

11 MĀRUTI: The monkey-god who helped Rāma in his quest for Sītā (the *Rāmāyana*). He is the son of Vāyu (the wind) and Bhīma's half-brother. He is the embodiment of knowledge, devotion, detachment and self-sacrifice.

12 VṚKODARA: One whose belly is like a wolf's – concave, with an immense appetite and digestive power. Bhīma possessed these characteristics and was therefore referred to by this name.

VRINDA NABAR

SELECT BIBLIOGRAPHY

Swami Abhedananda, *Doctrine of Karma*, R. Vedanta Math, Calcutta 1947

Theos Bernard, *Philosophical Foundations of India*, Rider, London 1945

Mahadeva Desai, *The Gītā According to Gandhi*, Navjivan Publishers, Ahmedabad 1946

Franklin Edgerton, *Bhagavadgītā*, Vol. II, Harvard University Press, London 1944

S. Radhakrishnan, *Indian Philosophy*, Vol. I, George Allen and Unwin, London 1941

S. Radhakrishnan (tr.), *The Bhagavadgītā*, Indus, New Delhi 1994

C. Kunhan Raja, *Some Fundamental Problems of Indian Philosophy*, Motilal Banarsidass, Delhi 1960

P. T. Raju, *Idealistic Thought of India*, George Allen and Unwin, London 1953

Ranade and Belvalkar, *History of Indian Philosophy*, Aryabhushan Publishers, Poona 1936

A. Schweitzer, *Indian Thought and Its Development*, Hodder, London 1936

Shashi Tharoor, *The Great Indian Novel*, Penguin India, New Delhi 1990 (an imaginative fictional application of the *Mahābhārata* to the twentieth-century Indian context)

B. G. Tilak, *Gītā Ranasya*, R. B. Tilak, Lokmanya Tilak Mandir, Poona 1936

THE BHAGAVADGĪTĀ

CHAPTER I

Yoga of the Hesitation and Dejection of Arjuna

Dhṛtarāṣṭra said:

1 O Sañjaya, what did my sons and the sons of Pāṇḍu do when, desiring war, they gathered together on the sacred field of Kurukṣetra?

Sañjaya said:

2 Having then seen the Pāṇḍava army standing drawn up, arrayed for battle, Prince Duryodhana went up to his ācārya [preceptor], Droṇa, and said:

3 Behold, O Master, this mighty army of the sons of Pāṇḍu, which has been marshalled by your talented pupil, the son of Drupada.

4 There are in it heroes – mighty bowmen who equal Bhīma and Arjuna in battle: Yuyudhāna, Virāṭa, and the great chariot warrior Drupada,

5 Dhṛṣṭaketu, Cekitāna, and the valiant king of Kāśī, Purujit, Kuntibhoja and Śaibya, the first among men,

6 The heroic Yudhāmanyu, and valiant Uttamaujā, as well as the son of Subhadrā and Draupadī's sons, great charioteers all of them.

7 I shall now mention, O best among the twice-born, the names of the most distinguished amongst us, the leaders of my army, for your information: know who they are.

8 Yourself, and Bhīṣma and Karṇa and Kṛpa, always victorious in battle, Aṣvatthāmā and Vikarṇa as well as the son of Somadatta.

9 And, moreover, many brave men who are risking their lives on my behalf. All of them are well equipped with various weapons and are well skilled in the art of warfare.

10 This army of ours, protected by Bhīṣma, is unlimited, while their army, guarded by Bhīma, is limited.

11 Therefore, now, do all of you assume positions in the respective ranks allotted to you, and protect Bhīṣma on all fronts.

12 To encourage him, the Kuru patriarch, his valiant grandsire, roared aloud like a lion, and blew his conch.

13 At this, conches, kettledrums, tabors, drums and cowhorns suddenly sounded forth and the noise of that was tumultuous.

14 Thereat, Mādhava [Kṛṣṇa] and the son of Pāṇḍu [Arjuna], who were seated in their magnificent chariot, to which were yoked white horses, blew their divine conches.

15 Hṛṣīkeśa [Kṛṣṇa] blew the Pāñcajanya, Dhananjaya [Arjuna] the Devadatta, and Vṛkodara, the performer of terrifying deeds [Bhīma], blew his mighty conch, the Pauṇḍra.

16 King Yudhiṣṭir, son of Kuntī, blew his Anantavijaya, and Nakula and Sahadeva the Sughoṣa and Maṇipuṣpaka.

17 Likewise the king of Kāśi, an excellent archer, Śikhaṇḍi, the great chariot-warrior, Dhṛṣṭadyumna, Virāṭa and Sātyaki, the invincible,

18 Drupada, and the sons of Draupadī, O ruler of the earth, and the mighty-armed son of Subhadrā, all these individually blew their respective conches on all sides.

19 That tumultuous uproar rent the hearts of the sons of Dhṛtarāṣṭra as it reverberated through the earth and the sky.

20 Then, looking at the sons of Dhṛtarāṣṭra who were properly arrayed for battle, the Pāṇḍava [i.e. Arjuna] whose ensign depicts Māruti took up his bow just as the onslaught of weapons was about to start.

21 Then, O ruler of the earth, addressing Hṛṣīkeśa,

Arjuna said:

O Acyuta [one who is unperturbed/unshaken, Kṛṣṇa], please position my chariot between the two armies,

22 In order that I may awhile observe these people standing here, desirous of battle, as well as those with whom I shall have to fight in this war.

23 I wish to look upon those who have gathered here in order to fight for the evil-minded son of Dhṛtarāṣṭra, by achieving in battle what is dear to him.

Sañjaya said;

24 When thus requested by Gudākeśa [Arjuna], O Bhārata [Dhṛtarāṣṭra], Hṛṣīkeśa drew up that finest among chariots between the two armies.

25 Facing Bhīṣma and Droṇa and all the other rulers, he said: 'O Pārtha [Arjuna], look on all these Kurus gathered [here].'

26 And Arjuna saw, standing there, paternal uncles, grandfathers, teachers, maternal uncles, brothers, sons, grandsons and friends.

27 As also fathers-in-law and friends in both the armies. And when the son of Kuntī [Arjuna] saw that all those who had taken up their positions there were his kinsmen.

28 He was overwhelmed with compassion and spoke thus in sadness.

Arjuna said:

O Kṛṣṇa, when I see these people, my kinsmen assembled here, eager for battle,

29 My limbs sag, my mouth feels parched, my body quakes, and my hair stands on end.

30 The Gāṇḍiva [bow] slips from my hand, my whole body is hot. I am unable to stand still and my mind is in a whirl.

31 I see adverse omens, O Keśava, and do not foresee any good from killing my own kinsmen in battle.

32 I do not hanker for victory, O Kṛṣṇa, or for sovereignty, or pleasures. Of what use to us is having a kingdom, O Govinda [Kṛṣṇa], or enjoyment, or life itself?

33 Those for whose sake we desire kingdom, enjoyments and pleasures stand here for battle, having abandoned their lives and wealth.

34 Teachers, fathers, sons, grandfathers too; maternal uncles, fathers-in-law, grandsons and brothers-in-law and other kinsfolk:

35 These I would not wish to kill though they have risen to kill us, O Madhusūdana [Kṛṣṇa], even to obtain the kingdom of the three worlds; far less so for the sake of the earth.

36 What pleasure can be ours, O Janārdana [Kṛṣṇa], by killing the sons of Dhṛtarāṣṭra? Sin alone will take hold of us if we kill these wicked ones.

37 It is not proper, therefore, that we kill our kinsmen, the sons of Dhṛtarāṣṭra: indeed, having killed our own folk, how can we be happy, O Mādhava?

38 Though these, their minds overpowered by greed, see no guilt in the extinction of a family and no sin in treachery towards friends,

39 Why is it, O Janārdana, that we do not learn to recoil from this sin though we clearly perceive the guilt in annihilating a family?

40 In the annihilation of a family, its time-honoured rites are destroyed; and when these rites perish, lawlessness overpowers the entire family.

41 When lawlessness prevails, O Kṛṣṇa, the women of the family are corrupted: and when women grow corrupt, O Vārṣṇeya [Kṛṣṇa], it results in the confusion of castes.

42 And this confusion leads the family itself and those who have destroyed it to hell. And their ancestors fall as well, deprived of their ritual offerings of rice-balls and water.

43 On account of the sins of those who destroy the family and cause confusion of the varnas, the eternal rites of family and caste are destroyed.

44 And we have heard, O Janārdana, that those whose family-rites have been destroyed must needs reside in hell.

45 Alas! what a heinous sin we are prepared to commit in rising to kill our own kinsmen through greed for the pleasures of sovereignty.

46 If the sons of Dhṛtarāṣṭra, weapons in hand, were to kill me in battle while I am unarmed and unable to retaliate, it would be far better for me.

Sañjaya said:

47 Having spoken thus on the battlefield, Arjuna sat down on the seat of his chariot, casting aside his bow and arrow, his mind agitated with grief.

In the Upaniṣad of the *Bhagavadgītā*, the knowledge of Brahman the Supreme, the science of yoga, and the dialogue between Śrīkṛṣṇa and Arjuna,

THIS IS THE FIRST CHAPTER ENTITLED

'Yoga of the Hesitation and Dejection of Arjuna'

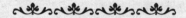

CHAPTER 2

Sāṃkhya Yoga

Sañjaya said:

1 To him [who was] in this way overwhelmed with pity, whose eyes were shadowed, filled with tears, and who was distressed, Madhusūdana spoke these words:

Śrī Bhagavān said:

2 O Arjuna, from where has this disgraceful conduct come into your mind in this hour of peril? It is unknown to the Āryas, does not lead to heaven, and brings one disrepute.

3 O Pārtha, do not give in to this unmanliness: it is unbecoming of you. Cast off this despicable faint-heartedness and stand up, O Vanquisher of foes.

Arjuna said:

4 O Madhusūdana , how shall I counter-attack with arrows in battle either Bhīṣma or Droṇa? They are worthy of great reverence, O Destroyer of foes.

5 It is better to live by begging in this world rather than by killing one's revered elders. Though aware of their gains, they are my elders, and by killing them, any worldly pleasures I enjoy will be tainted with blood.

6 We do not know which is the more meritorious for us – that we vanquish them or that they vanquish us. We would not care to live if we killed those who now stand before us for battle – the sons of Dhṛtarāṣṭra.

7 My natural temperament is weighed down with feeble pity. My mind is confused about my duty. I entreat You to tell me which is assuredly more meritorious. I am Your disciple and have surrendered myself to You: instruct me.

8 I see no means to remove this grief which parches my senses, though I were to win a prosperous and unrivalled kingdom on earth or even the sovereignty of the gods.

Sañjaya said:

9 Having spoken thus to Hṛṣīkeśa, the powerful Guḍākeśa, Vanquisher of foes, fell silent, saying this to Govinda: 'I shall not fight.'

10 Then, O Bhārata, Hṛṣīkeśa – smiling as it were – spoke these words to him who sat dejected amidst two armies.

Śrī Bhagavān said:

11 You grieve for those whom you should not grieve for, and yet you talk about wisdom! The wise do not lament either the dead or the living.

12 There was never a time when either I, or you, or these rulers of men did not exist. Nor will there ever be a future when all of us will cease to exist.

13 Just as in this corporeal form the soul experiences infancy, youth and old age, so does it in taking on another body. The wise man has no doubts about this.

14 Sensory contacts, O Son of Kuntī, which produce cold and heat, pleasure and pain, come and go. They are impermanent, O Bhārata, learn to bear them.

15 O Chief among men [Arjuna], it is the wise man who is not affected by them, who is the same in pain and pleasure, who becomes fit to attain immortality.

16 That which does not exist [*asat*] can have no becoming, while that which exists [*sat*] can never cease to be. The seers of truth have perceived this about the essence of things.

17 Know that that which has pervaded the world is indestructible. No one can bring about the destruction of the Immutable.

18 It is these bodies, acquired by the eternal, indestructible and unimaginable embodied [soul], which are said to come to an end. Fight, therefore, O Bhārata.

19 He who thinks that it [the embodied soul] kills or he who thinks that it is killed: both these do not possess the truth. It neither kills nor is killed.

20 It is never born, nor does it ever die. Nor, having once existed, will it cease to do so. It is unborn, eternal, immutable and primeval. It is not killed though the body is slain.

21 How, O Pārtha, can a person who realises that it is indestructible, eternal, unborn and unchanging, kill anyone, or cause anyone to kill?

22 Just as a man casts off worn-out clothes and puts on others which are new, likewise the embodied soul, casting off old bodies, is united with other, new ones.

23 Weapons do not cut it; fire does not burn it; water does not wet it; the wind does not dry it.

24 It is uncleavable, and cannot be burnt, wetted or dried. It is permanent, all-pervading, stable, immovable and primordial.

25 It is said to be imperceptible, unthinkable and unchanging. Therefore, knowing it to be so, it does not become you to grieve.

26 Even if you believe that it is constantly born and constantly dies, even so, O Mighty-armed, it does not become you to grieve.

27 For to one that is born death is certain, and to one that dies, birth is certain. This being unavoidable, you ought not to grieve.

28 O Bhārata, all created beings are unmanifest in their beginning, manifest in the middle, and unmanifest again in death. Then what is there to lament over?

29 Some behold it [the Ātman] as a wonder, others speak of it as a wonder. Still others hear of it as a wonder. But even after all this, not one of these has known it.

30 That which dwells in every body [the Ātman] and is its owner is eternal and indestructible, O Bhārata. It is not proper therefore for you to lament over any creature.

31 Moreover, even if you regard your own duty, you should not falter: there is nothing more meritorious for a Kṣatriya than warfare prescribed by duty.

32 And such a war, O Pārtha, which is indeed like an open door to heaven, comes unsought only to those Kṣatriyas who are fortunate.

33 But if you do not fight this righteous battle, you will have failed in your duty, lost your honour, and incurred sin.

34 Moreover, men will always narrate your infamy and, to one who has been held in high esteem, infamy is worse than death.

35 The great chariot-warriors will think that you withdrew from war through fear, and they who held you in high esteem will think less of you.

36 Your enemies, scorning your strength, will say many unmentionable things. Can there be anything more painful than that?

37 If killed, you will attain heaven; if victorious, you will enjoy the earth. Therefore arise, O Son of Kuntī, intent on battle.

38 Then, regarding as alike pleasure and pain, gain and loss, victory and defeat, prepare yourself for battle. If you act thus, you shall not incur sin.

39 This wisdom, given to you, is of the Sāṁkhya system. Now, O Pārtha, listen to the wisdom of the Yoga, possessed of which, you shall cast off the bondage of action.

40 Along this path, no action begun is ever frustrated, and no obstacles arise. Even a little of this dharma preserves one from grave danger.

41 Along it, O Descendant of the Kurus [Arjuna], that Reason which can discern between the dos and don'ts is unwavering, but the fancies of those whose Reason is not resolute are many-branched and endless.

42 O Pārtha, the dull-witted who are enamoured of the panegyrics in the Vedas and assert that there is nothing else [of consequence], mouth flowery words about

43 Specific rites whose fruit is rebirth and the attainment of pleasure and power. And those who, minds filled with desire, regard attainment of heaven as their highest reward,

44 Are carried away by these words, becoming immersed in pleasure and power: in them that Reason that discerns between right and wrong can never be fixed in concentration.

45 The Vedas cover only the three constituents of action. Transcend the three, O Arjuna. Be free from the dualities [opposites], always firm in goodness, unconcerned with acquisition and preservation, and centred in the Self.

46 To the extent that one needs a well when a place is flooded with water, just so will the enlightened Brahmin need the Vedas [specifically that part of the Vedas which contains the Karma-Kāṇḍa, prescribing rituals].

47 You have a right to the performance of action alone, its fruits are never within your control. Do not perform action with an eye to its fruits, nor let there be in you any attachment to the non-performance of action.

48 O Dhanañjaya, casting off attachment, perform action being steady in its yoga, accepting alike success or failure. Such equanimity is known as yoga [i.e. Karma Yoga].

49 Mere action is by far inferior to the yoga of wisdom [i.e. action performed in wisdom]. O Dhanañjaya, take refuge in wisdom. Those who seek the fruits [of action] are to be pitied.

50 He who is fixed in wisdom remains untouched by either sin or merit here. Therefore, take refuge in yoga, for yoga means skill in performing action.

51 The wise who act in union [with the divine], abandoning the fruits of action and released from the fetters of births [i.e. successive rebirths], reach the state where there is no sorrow.

52 When your understanding has traversed the turbid enclosure of ignorance, you will become indifferent to what may have been heard or is yet to be heard.

53 When your understanding, now confused by Vedic statements, becomes fixed and stable in the state of samadhi [mental absorption], then will you attain yogic insight.

Arjuna said:

54 How would one describe the man who has this steady Reason, who is steeped in mental absorption, O Keśava? How would a man of fixed intelligence speak, sit or walk?

Śrī Bhagavān said:

55 O Pārtha, when a man relinquishes all the desires of his mind, and when his spirit delights in itself, then is he called a man of steady wisdom.

56 He whose heart is unperturbed in the midst of calamities and free from longing in the midst of pleasures, from whom attachment, fear and rage have departed, is called a sage of steady reason.

57 He who is unattached in all things, who neither exults in nor feels aversion for any good or evil that befalls him, is said to be steady in his wisdom.

58 When a person withdraws his senses from the objects of sense on every side the way a tortoise draws in its limbs, his wisdom is steady.

59 The objects of sense abandon the man who abstains from feeding on them, but the longing for them does not cease. But even this relish ceases when he has experienced the Supreme.

60 O Son of Kuntī, these turbulent senses lead away by force the mind of even the wise man who is striving [for control].

61 Having acquired self-control, he should sit in yoga and meditate on Me alone. He whose senses are thus controlled is steady in his wisdom.

62 A man who contemplates the objects of sense develops an attachment to them; attachment gives rise to desire, and desire results in anger.

63 Anger gives rise to confusion, confusion to loss of memory. Loss of memory destroys intelligence and, once a man's intelligence is destroyed, he perishes.

64 But the man whose mind is disciplined and whose senses are under control is free from attachment and aversion though he moves among the objects of sense, and such a person attains serenity.

65 And in that serenity, all his misery is destroyed; because the intelligence of the man of serenity is also steadied immediately.

66 A man whose senses are not under control cannot acquire knowledge; nor can he meditate. A man who cannot meditate cannot acquire tranquillity and, for the man who lacks tranquillity, how can there be happiness?

67 The mind which pursues the wandering senses carries off man's Reason the way a gale carries off a ship on the waters.

68 Therefore, O Mighty-armed, he whose senses are controlled from the objects of sense is steady in his wisdom.

69 The man of self-control is awake when it is night for all creatures; and such a sage sees as night that in which all other creatures are awake.

70 True peace is obtained only by him in whom all objects of sense enter the way waters enter the sea, filling it on all sides without disturbing its shores – not by one who desires these objects.

71 He who acts after giving up all desire, who is free from any sort of 'mineness' or egoism, he alone attains tranquillity.

72 O Pārtha, this is the Brāhmic state. Having attained it, man is not left in ignorance. Steady in that state even at the end [i.e. the moment of death], he acquires release through merging with the Brahman.

In the Upaniṣad of the *Bhagavadgītā*, the knowledge
of Brahman the Supreme, the science of yoga,
and the dialogue between Śrīkṛṣṇa and Arjuna,
THIS IS THE SECOND CHAPTER ENTITLED
'Sāṁkhya Yoga'

CHAPTER 3

Karma Yoga: The Way of Action

Arjuna said:

1 O Janārdana, if you are of the opinion that wisdom is superior to action, why then, O Keśava, do you exhort me to perform this terrible act?

2 With this apparently conflicting advice, it is as if you confuse my understanding. Tell me for certain, therefore, that one thing by which I would attain bliss.

Śrī Bhagavān said:

3 O sinless one, I have said earlier [in Chapter 2] that the way in this world is two-fold: the path of knowledge [Jñāna Yoga] for those who contemplate and that of doing [Karma Yoga] for those who act.

4 A man does not attain release from action by not acting, nor does he attain perfection by mere renunciation of action.

5 For, no matter who he is, he cannot remain for even a moment without acting. Prakṛti [impulses born of nature] compels everyone who is dependent to keep performing action.

6 The deluded one who keeps in check the organs which act while continuing in his mind to brood over the objects of sense is termed a hypocrite.

7 But the man who controls his senses with his mind and, with detachment, begins his Karma Yoga using the organs of action, is, O Arjuna, a very worthy man.

8 Perform the action prescribed for you, because it is better to act than to be inactive. Without action, even the maintenance of your body will be impossible.

9 Except for work performed in the spirit of sacrifice, all other holds the world in bondage. Therefore, O Son of Kuntī, perform your action in the spirit of sacrifice, free from any form of attachment.

10 In ancient times, the Lord of Creation created all living beings along with sacrifice, saying, 'May you grow [multiply] out of this, and may it be to you that which will fulfil all your desires.'

11 By it, please the gods, and let them please you. Pleasing each other thus, may you attain supreme good.

12 Pleased with the sacrifice, the gods will grant you your desired enjoyments. He who enjoys what they have given without giving to them in return is indeed a thief.

13 The good who partake of the remains of the sacrifice are redeemed from all sins, but the sinful who cook food for themselves alone partake of sin.

14 Beings are born of food; food is produced from rain; rain results from sacrifice; and sacrifice results from action [karma].

15 Know the origin of action [karma] to be in Brahman, and that Brahman has sprung from the Imperishable. Therefore this Brahman, which is all-pervading, is always the primary focus of sacrifice.

16 The man who does not help to turn the wheel which has thus been set in motion in this world is full of sin, and the life, O Pārtha, of him who is a slave to the senses is worthless.

17 But the man merged only with the Self [the Ātman], content in the Self, pleased with it, has no action that needs to be performed.

18 Similarly, he has nothing to gain here either by doing or not doing; nor does he depend upon any created being for attaining any purpose.

19 Therefore, always perform what you have to do without attachment, for the man who performs action without attachment attains the highest state.

20 It was through performing action that Janaka and others also attained release. Likewise, it is fitting that you also act bearing in mind the welfare of the world.

21 Whatever a great man does is also done by ordinary people. The world follows whatever norm he sets.

22 O Pārtha, I have no duty left to perform in the three worlds. There is nothing left unattained which I have to attain. Yet, I am engaged in action.

23 For if I do not engage in action without idleness, then, O Pārtha, all men follow My path in every respect.

24 If I cease to work, these worlds would grow extinct. I shall be the cause of the world's disarray and destroy these people.

25 Therefore, O Bhārata, as the ignorant perform action being attached to it, the wise should perform action unattached, desiring to maintain the welfare of the world.

26 The wise man should not unsettle the faith of the ignorant one's attachment to action, but should himself become a doer of deeds in the spirit of yoga, and enjoin others to do so willingly .

27 Though all actions are done by the constituents of nature [prakṛti], the ignorant one, deluded by his egoism, regards himself as the doer.

28 But, O Mighty-armed, he who realises that these constituents and the actions are both distinct from himself, and that it is only the constituents interacting together, does not grow attached.

29 People who are deluded by the constituents of prakṛti get attached to the actions they produce. Such imperfect, dull-witted people should not be unsettled by the wise.

30 Surrendering all actions to Me, with your mind fixed in the Self, freed from desire and the idea of ownership, fight, delivered from your mental fever.

31 The devout who, without finding fault with My teaching, always act according to it, are also freed from [the bondage of] karma [action].

32 But know that those who fault My teaching and do not follow it, are foolish beyond redemption, thoughtless, and are utterly ruined.

33 Even the wise man acts according to his own nature. All created beings follow their own inclination. Then what use is restraint?

34 There is a fixed order of attraction and repulsion between each sense and its object. Let no one come under their domination, for they are marauding enemies of men.

35 One's own dharma [code], imperfect though it may be, is better than the dharma of another, however well discharged. It is better to die engaged in one's own dharma, for it is risky to follow the dharma of another.

Arjuna said:

36 O Vārṣṇeya, now tell me, why is man impelled to commit sin as though he were forced to, even against his will?

Śrī Bhagavān said:

37 This is desire, this is anger, born out of the *rajas* constituent [passion], all-consuming and all-sinful. Know this as the enemy here.

38 Just as fire is covered by smoke, a mirror by dust, an embryo enveloped by the womb, so is everything covered by it.

39 O Son of Kuntī, this insatiable fire of desire, a constant enemy of the wise, has enveloped all wisdom.

40 The senses, the mind and the intellect are said to be its seat. With their support, it covers knowledge and throws man into confusion.

41 Therefore, O first among Bhāratas, control your senses first, and destroy this sinful slayer of spiritual knowledge and realisation.

42 It is said that the senses are great, that the mind is superior to the senses, the intellect to the mind, but that the Self is superior to the intellect.

43 Thus knowing that which is beyond the intellect, and controlling your self [your mind] by the Self, O Mighty-armed, destroy this foe in the shape of desire which is difficult to conquer.

In the Upaniṣad of the *Bhagavadgītā*, the knowledge of Brahman the Supreme, the science of yoga, and the dialogue between Śrīkṛṣṇa and Arjuna,

THIS IS THE THIRD CHAPTER ENTITLED

'Karma Yoga: The Way of Action'

CHAPTER 4

The Way of Knowledge and the Abandonment of Action

Śri Bhagavān said:

1 I expounded this inexhaustible yoga to Vivasvat; Vivasvat told it to Manu and Manu to Ikṣvāku.

2 Created through this oral tradition, this yoga was known to the royal sages till, O Vanquisher of foes [Arjuna], after a considerable lapse of time, it ceased to be in this world.

3 That same ancient yoga, the most supreme among mysteries, has been revealed by Me to you today because you are My devotee and friend.

Arjuna said:

4 Your birth was later, and that of Vivasvat came earlier. Then, how am I to understand that You had expounded it to him at first?

Śrī Bhagavān said:

5 I have lived through many past lives as have you, O Arjuna ; I know them all but you do not know them, O Vanquisher of foes.

6 Though free from all births, and though My own Self never suffers change, though Lord of all created things, even so, governing My own nature, I take birth through My own Māyā.

7 Whenever righteousness declines and unrighteousness grows powerful, then, O Bhārata, I manifest Myself.

8 I come into being from age to age to protect the good, destroy the wicked and establish righteousness.

9 He who grasps the essence of these transcendental births and actions is not reborn when he sheds his body but attains Me, O Arjuna.

10 Freed from love, fear and anger, devoted to Me, seeking shelter in Me, many people purified by the penance of knowledge have attained My Being.

11 In whatever way men worship Me, accordingly I requite them. O Pārtha, men follow My path in all [manner of] ways.

12 Men who desire the fruits of action offer sacrifices to the deities, because the fruit of such action is quickly got in this world of men.

13 The order of the four varṇas was created by Me in accordance with the differences in their qualities and actions. Though its creator, know me as the non-doer, Immutable.

14 Neither do actions smear Me nor do I crave for their fruits. He who knows Me in this light is not bound by action.

15 Knowing this, the ancient seekers of liberation performed their duties. You too, therefore, undertake action as was done by the ancients in the past.

16 Even the wise are confused as to what constitutes action [*karma*] and what inaction [*akarma*]. I shall explain that action [*karma*] to you, knowing which you shall be freed from sin.

17 One needs to know what is meant by action, to know the wrong kind of action, and what is inaction. The way of karma is inscrutable.

18 He who sees inaction in action and action in inaction is the sage among men. He practises yoga and performs all actions.

19 He whose actions are free from all desire for fruit, whose actions are reduced to ashes in the fire of wisdom, is called a learned man by the wise ones.

20 Having renounced attachment to action and its fruit, always happy, depending on nothing, he does nothing though always engaged in action.

21 Having given up desire, regulating his heart and mind, becoming free from all attachments, performing actions which are merely physical in nature, he does not commit sin.

22 He who is satisfied with whatever falls his way, who is free from the dualities [of pleasure and pain], without jealousy, the same whether he is successful in action or not, is not bound even when he acts.

23 A man without attachments, who is free, his mind focused in knowledge, and who performs action in the spirit of sacrifice, his action melts away completely.

24 To him, the act of offering is Brahman; the oblation is Brahman; it is offered by Brahman into the holy fire which is Brahman. He who sees Brahman in his action alone attains Brahman.

25 Some yogins offer sacrifices to the deities, while others make of the sacrifice itself a sacrifice into the fire of Brahman.

26 Some sacrifice hearing and other senses into the fire of restraint, others sacrifice sound and other objects of sense in the fire of the senses.

27 Still others offer all the actions of their senses and of the vital forces into the fire of the yoga of mental control, which has been set alight by knowledge.

28 Similarly, some sacrifice their wealth, others through austerity or yogic practices, while some sages of severe vows who have subdued their minds offer their study and knowledge.

29 Others who are dedicated to breath control, controlling the movement of prāṇa [the outgoing breath] and apāna [the incoming breath], sacrifice prāṇa into apāna or apāna into prāṇa.

30 Others again, limiting their food, sacrifice their prāṇa into prāṇa. All these are well versed in sacrifice and, through sacrifice, have had their sins destroyed.

31 And these, eating the amṛta, the remains of the sacrifice, attain the eternal Brahman. This world is not for the one who performs no sacrifice: how then any other, O best among the Kurus [Arjuna]?

32 In this way, various forms of sacrifice are set forth in the mouth of the Brahman. Know that all these issue from action, for when you know this you shall be released.

33 O Vanquisher of foes, sacrifice performed by offering everything into the fire of knowledge is superior to any material sacrifice. For, O Pārtha, all actions, without exception, are finally merged in knowledge.

34 Bear in mind that the wise who have seen the truth will instruct you in knowledge if you show humility in reverence, inquiry and service.

35 Having known it, O Pāṇḍava, you shall not again be subject to such confusion, for by means of it you shall see all created things as located in your Self and then in Me.

36 Even if you are the greatest among all sinners, you shall sail across all sin in this bark of wisdom.

37 As kindled fire reduces all fuel to ashes, likewise, O Arjuna, does the fire of knowledge reduce all action to ashes.

38 There is nothing in this world as purifying as knowledge. He who has mastered yoga discovers this of his own accord in his self in course of time.

39 The man of faith who, having disciplined his senses, pursues knowledge, attains it, and having gained it, immediately attains the supreme peace.

40 But the man without either knowledge or faith, who has a doubting mind, is wholly destroyed. For the one who doubts, there is neither this world, nor the one after, nor any kind of happiness.

41 O Dhanañjaya, actions cannot bind the man who has cast off all action through yoga, whose doubts have been destroyed by knowledge, and who has realised his self.

42 Therefore, cutting apart with the sword of knowledge this doubt which has arisen in your heart through ignorance, take refuge in yoga and stand up, O Bhārata.

In the Upaniṣad of the *Bhagavadgītā*, the knowledge
of Brahman the Supreme, the science of yoga,
and the dialogue between Śrīkṛṣṇa and Arjuna,
THIS IS THE FOURTH CHAPTER ENTITLED
'The Way of Knowledge and the Abandonment of Action'

CHAPTER 5

The Yoga of Renunciation

Arjuna said:

1 You now praise the path of renunciation, O Kṛṣṇa, and then again the path of unselfish action. Tell me for sure which of these two is more meritorious.

Śrī Bhagavān said:

2 Both renunciation of action and its selfless performance lead to salvation, but of the two, the selfless performance of action is superior to its renunciation.

3 He who has neither hate nor desire should be regarded as a perpetual ascetic; for liberated from these dualities, O Mighty-armed, he is effortlessly freed from bondage.

4 The foolish say that sāṁkhya [renunciation] and yoga [i.e. Karma Yoga, performance of action] are different; the wise do not say so. He who follows any one path properly attains the fruit of both.

5 The state achieved by those who follow the path of renunciation is also achieved by men of action. He who sees that the ways of renunciation and of action are one has seen [the truth].

6 But renunciation, O Mighty-armed, is difficult to acquire in the absence of yoga; that sage who is immersed in yoga soon attains the Brahman.

7 He who is disciplined in the way of action, whose soul is pure, who has mastered his self and his senses, whose soul has become the soul of all created beings, is untainted by actions even though he acts.

8 He who has understood the divine principles and is disciplined in yoga realises 'I do nothing', and in seeing, hearing, touching, smelling, eating, walking, sleeping, breathing,

9 Speaking, excreting, taking, opening and shutting the eyes, believes that only the senses act among their respective objects.

10 He who acts without attachment, surrendering his works to the Brahman, is untouched by sin like a lotus-leaf by water.

11 Men of action perform all action without attachment, merely using the body, or mind, or reason, or senses, for self-purification alone.

12 The man disciplined in yoga attains total tranquillity by renouncing all desire for the fruits of action, while he who is not yet disciplined is attached to the fruit because of desire and is bound.

13 The embodied who has won full control over the senses, and has mentally renounced all action, lives at ease in this city of nine gates, neither acting nor causing work to be done.

14 The Supreme One does not create for men either the capacity for action or their actions. He does not link actions to their fruits. It is nature which performs this.

15 The all-pervading Soul does not acquire the merit or sin of anyone. Since wisdom is veiled by ignorance, all creatures are confused.

16 But those whose ignorance has been destroyed by knowledge, their knowledge like the sun lights up the Highest Being.

17 Training their thought and intellect on It, finding their inner purpose in It, devoted to It alone, they reach to that state from where they do not return, their sins washed away by knowledge.

18 Sages view with the same eye a Brahmin with learning and humility, a cow, an elephant, a dog, or even an outcast.

19 Even here what is created is conquered by those whose mind is fixed in equality. For the Brahman is without flaw and equitable towards all. Hence such people are merged in the Brahman.

20 One should not be glad on getting what is desired nor sad should the undesired occur. He whose mind is thus steady and devoid of confusion, that knower of the Brahman is established in the Brahman.

21 He whose soul is not attached to external contacts finds that bliss which is in the Self. Such a man, disciplined in yoga through his union with Brahman, enjoys unending bliss.

22 Those pleasures arising out of contacts [with external objects] are only the origin of unhappiness, for they have a beginning and an end. O Son of Kuntī, a wise man does not delight in them.

23 He who can even here, before he relinquishes this body, resist the impulses of desire and anger, is the freed and happy man.

24 He who has thus found happiness within himself, who has also found his peace and light within, such a yogin has become godlike and attained the release that comes of being one with the Brahman.

25 Those sages whose sins have been dissolved, who have lost their dualities, who have achieved self-control and find happiness in the good of all, attain the release of being one with the Brahman.

26 Those austere souls who are free from desire and anger, who have controlled their minds and possess Self-knowledge, the blessedness of God surrounds them.

27 Putting out of him all sensory contacts, fixing his gaze between his eyebrows, balancing even the prāṇa and apāna between the nostrils,

28 That sage, who has controlled the senses, mind and reason, and, resolved upon release, has cast off desire, fear and anger – he is, so to say, perpetually freed.

29 And having thereby realised Me as the Recipient of all sacrifices and austerities, the Supreme Lord of all the spheres, the Friend of all creation, he attains peace.

In the Upaniṣad of the *Bhagavadgītā*, the knowledge
of Brahman the Supreme, the science of yoga,
and the dialogue between Śrīkṛṣṇa and Arjuna,
THIS IS THE FIFTH CHAPTER ENTITLED
'The Yoga of Renunciation'

CHAPTER 6

The Yoga of Meditation

Śrī Bhagavān said:

1 The man who performs what he should without looking to its fruit is the saṃnyāsin [one who follows the path of saṁnyās or renunciation] and yogin. He who does not light the sacred fire and performs no rites is neither of these.

2 Know that what is termed renunciation is the discipline of yoga, O Pāṇḍava, for no one can become a yogin unless he renounces his motivation.

3 To the sage who desires to acquire yoga, action is said to be the means, but having acquired yoga, peace of mind is then said to be the means.

4 When a man does not grow attached to the objects of sense or to actions, when he renounces all motivation, he is said to have acquired yoga.

5 A man should himself raise himself, and should not himself demean himself; for he himself is the friend of his self, and he himself its enemy.

6 For when a man has himself overcome himself, his self is a friend but he who does not know that self makes it into his enemy.

7 When, overcoming the self, one has attained tranquillity, one's Supreme Self remains focused, poised alike in heat and cold, pleasure and pain, honour and dishonour.

8 He whose soul is satisfied with the wisdom of spiritual knowledge, who has attained complete control over his senses and is unshakeable,

to whom a lump of earth, a stone and gold are the same, such a yogi is said to have attained realisation.

9 He whose attitude is the same towards benefactors, friends, foes, towards the neutral, impartial or hateful ones, relatives, saints and even sinners, is said to be of special merit.

10 The yogin should concentrate his mind on yoga constantly, remaining alone in a solitary place, his mind and body under his complete control, free from desires and material greed.

11 His seat should be firmly fixed in a clean place, neither too high nor too low, on the sacred kuṣa grass, covered with a deer-skin and over it a cloth.

12 Seated there, mind concentrated on one point, thought and senses under total control, he should practise yoga that the soul may be purified.

13 Holding his body, head and neck erect and still, looking intently at the tip of his nose, his glance unwavering,

14 Calm, unafraid, firm in the vow of celibacy, controlling his mind, he should stay seated, his mind fixed on Me in total concentration, with Me as his supreme goal.

15 Concentrating his mind in this way always, the yogin, his mind controlled, acquires that peace of the highest nirvāṇa which is found in Me.

16 But yoga is not for him, O Arjuna, who eats too much or nothing at all, nor for him who sleeps too much or keeps awake too much.

17 He who is moderate in food and play, disciplined in his actions, and controlled in sleep or keeping awake achieves a yoga which destroys all pain.

18 When the controlled mind is solely focused on the Self, freed from all desire, a man is said to be at peace.

19 The yogin who practises yoga of the Self, with his mind controlled, is very like a lamp in a windless place which does not flicker.

20 That state wherein the mind is at rest, controlled through the use of yoga, wherein himself sees his Self and rejoices in the Self,

21 Wherein he experiences that supreme bliss only realised by the intellect and unattainable by the senses and, steadied there, no longer diverges from the truth,

22 On acquiring which, he considers no attainment greater and, firm therein, is not dislodged by any sorrow, however great:

23 That state is known as viyoga, which severs the union with pain. This yoga must be resolutely practised, not allowing the mind to be discouraged.

24 Giving up all desires which arise from thought, controlling the senses on all sides with the mind,

25 He should gradually grow tranquil, his mind steadied with his resolve, and fixing his mind on the Self, not allow any other thought to enter it.

26 No matter what makes the flickering and unsteady mind go astray, he should hold it back, bringing it under the control of the Self alone.

27 That yogin whose mind is at peace attains the highest bliss; his passions quietened, himself untainted, he attains union with the Brahman.

28 In this way, always disciplining the self, the yogin becomes free of all sins and happily experiences the infinite bliss of union with the Brahman.

29 He whose self has thus become immersed in yoga, sees his Self existing in everything and all things in the Self. All around he sees the same thing.

30 The one who sees Me everywhere and sees all things in Me – I never abandon him, and he never abandons Me.

31 That yogin who bears in mind the union of all created things and worships Me abiding in all living things, whatever he may be doing, exists in Me.

32 O Arjuna, the yogin who looks on everything in the same way as if it were his self, be it in pleasure or in pain, is held to be a perfect yogi.

Arjuna said:

33 O Madhusūdana, as I see it, this yoga which you proclaimed as acquired through a steady mind, does not have any lasting foundation because of inconstancy.

34 For the mind, O Kṛṣṇa, is unsteady, turbulent, powerful and obstinate. Controlling it, I think, is as difficult as enveloping the wind.

Śrī Bhagavān said:

35 O Mighty-armed, there can be no doubt that the mind is restless and difficult to subdue, but it can be subdued, O Son of Kuntī, through steady practice and detachment.

36 I hold that for the man whose mind is unsubdued, yoga is hard to achieve; but he whose mind is controlled can acquire it by trying through the right means.

Arjuna said:

37 He who is wanting in self-control, though possessed of faith, and whose mind, deflected from yoga, fails to acquire perfection in yoga, what does he attain, O Kṛṣṇa?

38 O Mighty-armed [Kṛṣṇa], estranged from both, surrounded by ignorance, failing to acquire stability in the path that leads to the Brahman, does he not split apart like a torn cloud?

39 You alone should remove completely this doubt of mine, O Kṛṣṇa, for no one else but you can dispel it.

Śrī Bhagavān said:

40 O Pārtha, neither in this world nor in the next does he come to grief; for, dear friend, never does a man who does good meet with a deplorable end.

41 Having reached the sphere of those who were righteous in deed and having lived there for many years, he who has fallen from the path of yoga is reborn in the home of those who are rich and pure in mind.

42 Or he is born in the family of yogins who are gifted with wisdom. Births like this are very rare in this world.

43 The spiritual impressions obtained in his earlier birth come back to him here, and from these he endeavours once more to attain perfection, O Descendant of the Kurus.

44 The practice of earlier births impels him irresistibly. The one who has known the urge to seek the knowledge of the yoga goes past the rule of the Vedas.

45 The yogi who perseveres constantly, absolved of his sins, attains success after many rebirths, and reaches the highest goal.

46 The yogin is superior to the ascetic; he is also superior to the man of knowledge and the man of action; therefore, Arjuna, you should become a yogin.

47 And among all yogins, he who worships Me possessing faith, his inner being surrendered to Me, I consider him the most complete of all.

In the Upaniṣad of the *Bhagavadgītā*, the knowledge
of Brahman the Supreme, the science of yoga,
and the dialogue between Śrīkṛṣṇa and Arjuna,
THIS IS THE SIXTH CHAPTER ENTITLED
'The Yoga of Meditation'

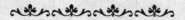

CHAPTER 7

The Way of Knowledge and Realisation

Śrī Bhagavān said:

1 O Pārtha, hear how you shall attain full and unquestionable knowledge of Me through practising yoga, concentrating your mind on Me, and taking refuge in Me.

2 I shall explain to you this wisdom along with knowledge, leaving nothing incomplete, knowing which there remains nothing left to know in this world.

3 Out of thousands of men, hardly one attempts to reach perfection, and among those who do so successfully, hardly one gains true knowledge of Me.

4 Earth, water, fire, air, ether, mind, reason and sense of self: these are the eight divisions of My nature.

5 This nature is of a lower order. O Mighty-armed, know that there exists, besides, My other superior nature, which is the essence by which the world is maintained.

6 Realise that all created beings take birth in both these. I am the origin of this cosmos and also its end.

7 O Dhanañjaya, there is nothing else higher than Me. Like a row of beads strung together, so is all which is here strung on Me.

8 I am the flavour in the water, O son of Kuntī; I am the radiance in the moon and the sun; I am the *aumkāra* in all the Vedas; I am the sound in ether as also manhood in all men.

9 I am the pure scent in the earth, the brilliance in fire; I am the life in all living beings. I am the austerity in ascetics.

10 O Pārtha, know Me as the eternal seed in all created things. I am the intelligence of the intelligent, and the magnificence of the magnificent.

11 I am the strength of all the strong, without their desire or attachment. I am also that desire in all created beings which is not inimical to morality.

12 And know likewise that all the objects of *sattva*, *rajas* and *tamas* have arisen from Me, but I am not in them, they are in Me.

13 Being confused by the three *guṇas*, which embody the three states, the entire universe does not realise Me, who am beyond these and inexhaustible.

14 This is My divine Māyā, an embodiment of these states of the *guṇas*, and difficult to comprehend. Therefore, only those who surrender to Me, can swim through this Māyā.

15 The foolish and those who perform evil, whose wisdom has been destroyed by Māyā, and who are infused with the reasoning of demons, do not surrender to Me.

16 Of four kinds are the virtuous people who worship Me, Arjuna, best of the Bhāratas – those in distress, those who seek knowledge, those who seek wealth, and the men of knowledge.

17 Of them, the highest in worth is that man of knowledge who regards worship of Me as the sole form of worship, and whose conduct is ever without desire. I am the most beloved of the man of knowledge and he of Me.

18 All of them are good, but I regard the man of knowledge as equal to Me. For having united his mind in Me he is fixed in Me, the highest goal.

19 Many births later, the man of knowledge, empirically concluding that all that is is Vāsudeva, comes and merges in Me. Such a noble soul is extremely rare.

20 There are people whose desires delude them, who worship other deities and practise various rites according to their individual natures.

21 Whatever form or deity a devotee with faith may wish to worship, I make his faith unswerving.

22 Imbued with that faith, he engages in the worship of that deity, and obtains from him the fruits which he desires and which I Myself have created.

23 But the fruit obtained by myopic men does not last. The ones who worship deities go to them, while My devotees come to Me.

24 Those without wisdom regard Me, who am imperceptible, as being perceptible, failing to realise My superior, supreme, immutable form.

25 Being enveloped in My mysterious power [Yoga-Māyā], I am not manifest to all. The ignorant do not realise that I am unborn and immutable.

26 I know all created beings in the past and present, O Arjuna, and those that will be, but no one knows Me.

27 All creatures in the world are immersed in ignorance, O Bhārata, the result of the delusion caused by the dualities arising from desire and hate, O Vanquisher of foes.

28 But the virtuous, whose sin has ended, escape from the ignorance caused by the dualities, worshipping Me with a firmness of purpose.

29 All those who shelter in Me, attempting to be free of old age and death, realise in full the Brahman, the Self and Action [*karma*].

30 Those who realise Me as existing in the physical plane, the divine planes, and also in what concerns sacrifices, have a mind which is focused and know Me even at the time of death.

In the Upaniṣad of the *Bhagavadgītā*, the knowledge
of Brahman the Supreme, the science of yoga,
and the dialogue between Śrīkṛṣṇa and Arjuna,
THIS IS THE SEVENTH CHAPTER ENTITLED
'The Way of Knowledge and Realisation'

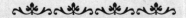

CHAPTER 8

The Yoga of the Immutable

Arjuna said:

1 What is that Brahman? What is Adhyātma [the Self]? And what is karma, O Puruṣottama [most excellent among persons]? What is that which is termed Adhibhūta? What is Adhidaiva?

2 What is the meaning of Adhiyajña and who is in this body, Madhusūdana ? How do the self-controlled realise You at the time of their death?

Śrī Bhagavān said:

3 Brahman is the immutable, the supreme element. The essence of each created being is the Adhyātma [the Self]. The creative force which brings forth all created things is called Karma.

4 Adhibhūta is the *kṣara* state [which is circumscribed by virtue of name and form and is mutable]; the Adhidaivata is the Puruṣa [the basic principle of the divine in the cosmos]; and the Adhiyajña [the basis of all sacrifices] is Myself, here in the body, O most exalted among embodied beings [Arjuna]!

5 And he who thinks of Me only at the time of his death and passes away, leaving his body, is merged in My being: there is no doubt about that.

6 Whatever form a man thinks of when, at the time of death, he leaves the body, that is the form which he attains, O Son of Kuntī, because he has ever been absorbed in thinking of it.

7 Therefore, remember Me at all times, and fight. Having concentrated your mind and intellect on Me, you will without a doubt come and be merged in Me.

8 A man who steadies his mind with the aid of discipline and practice, not allowing it to stray elsewhere, and meditates on the Supreme Divine Being, attains Him.

9 He who meditates on the one who is all-perceiving, the ancient, the ruler of all things, smaller than the atom, the supporter of this universe, whose form is inconceivable, who is as radiant as the sun beyond the darkness,

10 And who, at the time of death, his mind steadied through devotion and the power of yoga, fixes his vital breath right between his eyebrows – he departs and is merged in that radiant Supreme Being.

11 I shall now briefly describe to you that state called *akṣara* [the Immutable] by those who know the Vedas, which ascetics enter after freeing themselves from all wants and, desiring which, they observe the prescribed rites of austerity.

12 Controlling all the entrances, containing the mind within the heart, fixing one's life-breath in the head, steady, absorbed in yoga

13 And in the one-syllabled 'Aum', the form of Brahman, the one who thinks of Me as he leaves his body attains the highest state.

14 I am easily attainable, Pārtha, by that ever-restrained yogi who remembers Me every day and all the time, with his mind on nothing else.

15 Having attained Me, these noble souls are not subjected to that transitory abode of misery, rebirth, for they have attained the highest perfection.

16 Even from the sphere of Brahman and from all other spheres, there is sure to be a return to rebirth [in this world], Arjuna, but after having merged with Me, O Son of Kuntī, there is no rebirth.

17 Those who know that the day of Brahma ends after a thousand yugas, and likewise His night, know the essence of day and night.

18 All perceptible objects issue from the imperceptible at the start of this day, and when the night begins, they dissolve in the same imperceptible mentioned above.

19 This same multitude of beings being born again and again is dissolved at the start of night in spite of itself, O Pārtha, and is reborn at the approach of day.

20 But beyond this imperceptible there is yet another which is Imperceptible and Eternal and which does not end even with the end of all created beings.

21 That Imperceptible, said to be the Immutable, is held to be the Supreme Goal. Having attained this, there is no return. That is My supreme dwelling-place.

22 That Supreme Being, O Pārtha, within whom all creation is contained and by whom all this is pervaded, can only be attained by single-minded devotion.

23 I shall now reveal to you, O best of Bhāratas, that time of death in which yogins who die do not come back and also that in which they return.

24 Fire, radiance, day, the bright half [of the month], the six months of the northern solstice – the knowers of Brahman who depart during these attain the Brahman.

25 Smoke, night, the dark half, the six months of the southern solstice – the yogin who dies during these reaches the light of the moon and returns.

26 The light and the dark are held to be eternal paths of the world; he who goes by the one does not return; going by the other, he does.

27 O Pārtha, no yogin who knows these paths is ever deluded. Therefore, Arjuna, be fixed in yoga at all times.

28 Perceiving this, the yogin rises above the fruits of merit attached to the Vedas, sacrifices, austere practices and charity, reaching that primal state which is the highest.

In the Upaniṣad of the *Bhagavadgītā*, the knowledge
of Brahman the Supreme, the science of yoga,
and the dialogue between Śrīkṛṣṇa and Arjuna,
THIS IS THE EIGHTH CHAPTER ENTITLED
'The Yoga of the Immutable'

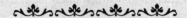

CHAPTER 9

The Yoga of Sovereign Knowledge and Sovereign Mystery

Śrī Bhagavān said:

1 Since you do not split hairs, I shall set forth for you this highly mysterious spiritual knowledge, along with the knowledge born of observation, possessed of which, you shall be delivered from sin.

2 This is the king of knowledge [*rājavidyā*], the sovereign mystery, supremely sanctifying, obtained through actual experience, consistent with dharma, easy to act on, and imperishable.

3 O Vanquisher of foes, men with no faith in this dharma do not attain Me, but return to the way of the mortal world.

4 I have pervaded this universe through My imperceptible form. All created things are in Me but I am not in them.

5 However, these created beings do not abide in Me. Behold this, My Divine Yoga. My spirit, which created these beings, is embodied in them but not in them.

6 Just as the great wind, blowing everywhere, is forever contained in space, likewise are all created beings in Me. Know this.

7 O Son of Kuntī, all created things are absorbed into My prakṛti at the end of a kalpa [one single day of Brahman; see Introduction, p. xii]; and, when a kalpa begins, I recreate them.

8 Seizing hold of my own prakṛti, I fashion again and again this great number of beings which is helpless [circumscribed by karma], being subject to prakṛti.

9 O Dhanañjaya, since I exist as if indifferent, unattached to My action, these actions do not bind Me.

10 Under My direction, prakṛti creates the movable and immovable universe. Because of this, O Son of Kuntī, the world keeps revolving.

11 The foolish do not respect Me in this human form, failing to know My supremely excellent form, that of the highest Lord of all creation.

12 Their desires are futile, their actions futile, their knowledge futile, their minds misled; they harbour an ignorant temperament, devilish and ungodly.

13 But, Pārtha, those noble souls who have sheltered in the divine nature, realising Me, the supreme inexhaustible source of all created beings, worship Me as if there is no one else.

14 Praising Me constantly, industrious and firm of purpose, prostrating with devotion before Me, always engrossed in yoga, they worship Me.

15 Others likewise, by means of ritualised knowledge, worship Me, who face all directions, as a synthesis of elements or by analysing My various parts.

16 I am the prescribed ritual; I am the sacrifice; I am the food offered to ancestors; I am the medicine prepared from plants; I am the sacrificial mantra; I am also the ghee; I am the Fire, and the offering thrown into the Fire is also Me.

17 I am the father, mother, supporter and grandfather of this world. I am all that makes holy or which can be known. I am the utterance 'Aum', and I am also the *rg.* , *sāma* and *yajur* [Vedas],

18 The ultimate state, the supporter, the lord, the witness, the dwelling, the refuge, the friend, the origin, the destruction, the existence, the place of repose and the imperishable seed.

19 I cause the heat of the sun, I hold back and release the rain; I am immortality as well as death, the imperishable and the perishable too, O Arjuna.

20 Those who perform the rituals in the three Vedas, the observers of the Soma-sacrifice, and the sinless, worshipping Me by means of sacrifices, pray that they may attain heaven. Reaching the holy sphere of Indra, they enjoy various divine pleasures in that heaven.

21 Having enjoyed the vast expanse of heaven, and their merit exhausted, they return to the mortal world. Thus, those who, desiring pleasure, adhere to the prescribed rites and rituals in the three Vedas, must needs go back and forth.

22 But those who think of nothing else and, meditating on Me, worship Me, always immersed in yoga, I look after their wellbeing and security.

23 Even those who become devotees of other deities and, with faith, perform sacrifices to them, they too sacrifice to Me, O Son of Kuntī, though not in the manner prescribed.

24 For I am the beneficiary and lord of all sacrifices. But, not understanding My true essence, they lapse.

25 Those who worship the deities go to the deities, ancestor-worshippers to the ancestors, those who worship spirits to the spirits, and those who worship Me reach Me.

26 Whoever with devotion offers Me a leaf, a flower, a fruit, or even some water, I accept the devotional offering of that man who has a regulated mind.

27 Whatever you do, whatever you eat, whatever you offer in sacrifice, whatever your gift, whatever austerity you observe, O Son of Kuntī, offer all that to Me.

28 In this way, you shall be free from those good and evil consequences which are the bonds of action. And, pure-hearted, finding release through that yoga which renounces the fruits of action, you will come and be merged in Me.

29 I am the same towards all creatures. To Me, no one is unliked or dear. But I am embodied in those who worship Me with devotion, and they in Me.

30 Even if he is a man of great evil, if he worships Me with unswerving faith, he must be regarded a saint, for what his reason has determined is right.

31 He soon becomes a soul imbued with dharma, and obtains eternal peace. O Son of Kuntī, know this for certain, that My devotee is never destroyed.

32 Because those who shelter in Me, O Pārtha, be they women, Vaiśyas, Śūdras, and others born in a sinful class, they too attain the highest bliss.

33 Then, even more so, the holy Brahmins and king-sages who are My devotees. Living in this impermanent and unhappy world, devote yourself to Me.

34 Fix your mind on Me; be My devotee; worship Me; make obeisance to Me; when you thus devote yourself to Me, and perform your yoga, you will reach Me, your final resort.

In the Upaniṣad of the *Bhagavadgītā*, the knowledge
of Brahman the Supreme, the science of yoga,
and the dialogue between Śrīkṛṣṇa and Arjuna,
THIS IS THE NINTH CHAPTER ENTITLED
'The Yoga of Sovereign Knowledge and Sovereign Mystery'

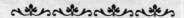

CHAPTER 10

The Yoga of Divine Manifestations

Śrī Bhagavān said:

1 Once more, O Mighty-armed, listen to My supreme message: I shall reveal it for your good, who have been made so happy [by My words].

2 Neither the pantheon of gods understands My origin nor the great sages for, in every way, I am the primary cause of the gods as well as the great sages.

3 He who perceives that I am without birth or origin, the great Īśvara [Supreme Lord] of all the spheres, he, among all mortal creatures, is freed of ignorance and freed from all sins.

4 Reason, knowledge, freedom from confusion, mercy, truth, self-restraint, tranquillity, happiness, unhappiness, being and non-being, fear and fearlessness,

5 Non-violence, evenness of temper, contentment, austerity, charity, glory, ill-repute – the different characteristics of living creatures – are born of Me.

6 The seven great sages as also the four of former times, and the Manus, from whom all living creatures are created in the world, are emanations of My mind.

7 He who realises the principle underlying My manifestation and My yoga in this is one with steady yoga; there is no doubt about this.

8 I am the origin of everything, all things issue forth from Me: realising this, the wise, imbued with My essence, worship Me.

9 Their minds on Me, their lives given up to Me, they counsel one another, talking about Me always, happy and absorbed in doing so.

10 On those who, constantly remaining content, worship Me with love, I bestow the yoga of discerning knowledge which aids them in coming to Me.

11 And, to bestow on them My care and concern, I enter their inner sense, destroying the darkness of ignorance with the glowing lamp of knowledge.

Arjuna said:

12 You are the Supreme Brahman, the Supreme State, Supremely Pure, the Permanent, Divine Being, First among the gods, the Unborn, the All-pervading.

13 This is said about You by all the sages, by the divine prophet Nārada too, and by Asita, Devala, even Vyāsa – and You Yourself say it to me.

14 I take to be true all that You tell me, O Keśava [Kṛṣṇa]. Neither the gods nor the demons know Your origin, O Lord.

15 You alone are the one who, through Yourself, know Yourself, O Supreme One, Creator and Lord of created beings, God of gods, Lord of the Universe.

16 Describe to me therefore, in every single detail, those divine manifestations of Yours by which, pervading these spheres, You exist.

17 How shall I come to know You, O yogin, by meditating on You continually? In what different forms should I, meditating, perceive You, O Blessed Lord?

18 Describe to me again, in detail, Your yoga and Your manifestations, O Janārdana: I cannot have enough of hearing Your nectar-like utterances.

Śrī Bhagavān said:

19 Very well, I shall describe to you My divine manifestations – the most significant among them – for, O best among the Kurus, there is no end to these My glories.

20 O Gudākeśa [Arjuna], I am the self located in the hearts of all created beings. I am also their origin, middle and final end.

21 Among the Ādityas I am Viṣṇu, the radiating sun among the bright bodies, the Marīci among the Maruts, the moon among the other stars.

22 Among the Vedas I am the Samāveda, Indra among the gods, the mind amid the senses, the conscious flow in created beings.

23 Among the Rudras I am Śaṁkara, Kubera among the Yakṣas and Rakṣasas, the Pāvaka of the Vasūs, the Meru among the mountain-peaks.

24 Among preceptors perceive Me, O Pārtha, as the primary one – Bṛhaspati; Skanda among the commanders of armies; the ocean among the waters.

25 Among the great sages I am Bhṛgu, in speech the single-syllabled 'Aum', the *japa-yajña* among the *yajñas*, the Himalaya among the immovable.

26 I am the Aśvattha among trees, the Nārada among divine ṛṣis, Citraratha among the gandharvas, the Kapila muni of souls who have perfected themselves.

27 Know Me also as the Uccaiśravas among horses, born of the churning of the ocean for nectar, the Airāvata among excellent elephants, the monarch among men.

28 I am the thunderbolt among weapons, the Kāmadhenu among cows, the God of sensual desire for the creators of progeny, Vāsuki among the serpents.

29 Among the Nāgas I am Ananta, Varuṇa among the water-gods, the Aryamā among ancestors, Yama among those who preserve the order.

30 I am the Prahlāda of the demons, Time among those who calculate it, the king among beasts [i.e. a lion], the son of Vinatā [Garuḍa, an eagle] among birds.

31 I am the wind among the swift, Rāma among those who wield weapons, the alligator among fishes, the Jāhnavi [Ganga] among rivers.

32 In all creation I am the beginning, the end and even the middle, O Arjuna, the knowledge of the Self among knowledges, the Speech of all those who debate.

33 I am the first vowel-sound [a] among letters, the dual among compounds. I am also the inexhaustible Time, the Giver who faces all directions.

34 I am Death, destroyer of all, and the origin of all that will be in the future. Among women, I am fame, prosperity, speech, memory, intelligence, firmness and mercy.

35 Among the Sāma, likewise, I am the Bṛhatsāma, the Gāyatrī among metres, the Mārgaśīrṣa among months, the flower-bearer [spring] among the seasons.

36 I am the gambling of the deceitful ones, the magnificence of the magnificent. I am victory, I am resolve, I am the constancy of the constant.

37 I am Vāsudeva among the Vṛṣṇis [Yadavas], Dhanañjaya [Winner of Wealth, Arjuna] among the Pāṇḍavas, Vyāsa too among the sages, and among poets the poet Uśanā.

38 Among those who chastise I am the rod, the statesmanship of those who wish for success, the silence of all that is mysterious, the knowledge of those who know.

39 Moreover, the seed of all that exists – that is Me, O Arjuna. Nor is there a single thing, movable or immovable, which can exist without Me.

40 There is no end to My divine manifestations, O Vanquisher of foes. What I have described is only a brief exposition of My limitless forms.

41 Whatever exists and is imbued with power, glory and magnificence, know that it has come out of a spark of My splendour.

42 But what is the point of your knowing all these details, O Arjuna? – I stand supporting the whole of this cosmos with a sole fragment of Myself.

In the Upaniṣad of the *Bhagavadgītā*, the knowledge
of Brahman the Supreme, the science of yoga,
and the dialogue between Śrīkṛṣṇa and Arjuna,
THIS IS THE TENTH CHAPTER ENTITLED
'The Yoga of Divine Manifestations'

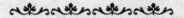

CHAPTER 11

The Yoga of the Revelation of the Cosmic Form

Arjuna said:

1 That supreme mysticism pertaining to the Self, which You expounded to show me favour, has made my ignorance leave me.

2 From You, whose eyes are like lotus-leaves, I have heard at length about the origin and passing away of all created beings, and also about Your inexhaustible grandeur.

3 O Supreme Lord, You have proclaimed Yourself to be thus; and thus, O Best of Persons, do I desire to see Your divine form.

4 O Lord, if You hold that it is possible for me to behold it, then, O Lord of Yoga, show me Your imperishable form.

Śrī Bhagavān said:

5 O Pārtha, look upon these hundreds and thousands of My forms, of various kinds, divine, of various colours and dimensions.

6 Look upon these Ādityas, the Vasus, the Rudras, the Aśvins, and also the Maruts. Look upon these numerous wonders, never before seen by you, O Bhārata.

7 Behold here today the entire universe, movable and immovable, and whatever else you desire to see, O Gudakesa, all collected in My form.

8 But you cannot view Me with these eyes of yours. I am bestowing supernatural sight on you – behold My divine yoga.

Sañjaya said:

9 O King, having spoken in this way, the Great Lord of Yoga, Hari, revealed the Supreme Divine Form to Pārtha:

10 Many mouths and eyes, many marvellous sights, many gleaming ornaments, many war-weapons, erect, shining,

11 Clad in divine garlands and garments, anointed with heavenly fragrance, containing every kind of marvel, a divine being without end, facing all directions.

12 Were the radiance of a thousand suns to blaze forth at one go in the sky, it might approximate the magnificence of this exalted being.

13 The Pāṇḍava then beheld the entire universe with its multiple divisions composed into a single system in this Body of the God of gods.

14 Then, wonder-struck, hair standing on end, palms joined and raised to his forehead, Dhanañjaya bowed to the Lord and said:

Arjuna said:

15 O Lord, I see in Your body all the gods as also the varied multitudes of created beings, Brahma the Supreme seated on the lotus-seat, all the ṛṣis [sages] and the glistening serpents.

16 I behold Your numberless arms, bellies, mouths and eyes, Your form infinite on all sides, but I do not perceive Your end, or Your middle or beginning, O Lord of the Cosmos, O Cosmic Form.

17 Your diadem, mace and discus, Your radiance glowing everywhere, a mountain of brilliance, I behold You who are impossible to behold, unbearably hot with the dazzle of fire and sun on all sides, limitless.

18 In my opinion, You are the Imperishable, the Supreme among what can be known, the Ultimate haven of the universe, the imperishable protector of the eternal dharma, and the Fundamental principle.

19 I see You as having no beginning, middle or end, with inexhaustible power, innumerable arms, the moon and sun for Your eyes, Your mouth a blazing fire, heating up this world with Your self-engendered radiance.

20 The space between the heavens and the earth has been pervaded by You alone, and likewise all its corners. Seeing this, Your wondrous terrible form, O Exalted Being, the three spheres are agitated.

21 Behold these hosts of gods entering Your body, some praying to You, in fear, with folded hands. And multitudes of great ṛṣis and beings who have perfected themselves hail You, praising You with sublime hymns.

22 The Rudras, the Ādityas, the Vasus and the Sādhyas, the Viśvas, the Aśvins, the Maruts, the ancestors, the bands of Gandharvas, the Yakṣas, Asuras and Siddhas, being mazed, are all looking at You.

23 Seeing Your huge form, O Mighty-Armed, with its many mouths and eyes, its many arms, thighs, feet, bellies, terrible with its many teeth, the worlds quake and so do I.

24 On seeing You touching the sky, lit up, many-hued, mouth opened wide, enormous lustrous eyes, the inmost part of me is agitated, and I have in me neither steadfastness nor peace, O Viṣṇu!

25 And seeing Your mouths, terrible with their many rows of teeth, which resemble the destructive flames of Time, I lose my sense of direction and obtain no tranquillity. O God of gods, Pervader of the Cosmos, be merciful!

26 All those sons of Dhṛtarāṣṭra, along with the multitudes of kings, and Bhīṣma, Droṇa and the Sūtputra [Karṇa], as well as the principal warriors on our side,

27 Are speedily entering Your frightening mouths with their terrible rows of teeth. The heads of some, being caught between Your teeth, are seen being crushed to powder.

28 Like the many coursing currents of the rivers race towards the ocean, so do these brave ones from the world of men charge into Your several blazing mouths.

29 Like moths leap swiftly into a flaming fire only to die there, likewise these men rush into Your mouths with great speed to be destroyed.

30 You swallow up all these people on every side, licking at them with Your blazing mouths. Your fiery heat pervades the whole universe, O Viṣṇu, singeing it with its burning radiance.

31 Tell me who You are, that have a form so terrible. I prostrate before You, most excellent among Gods, be merciful. I desire to know You, the Fundamental Spirit, for I do not understand what You have performed.

Śrī Bhagavān said:

32 I am Time, the destroyer of worlds, matured, and occupied now in destroying the world. Even were you not here, all the warriors, standing variously arrayed in the different armies, shall be no more.

33 Therefore, arise and obtain glory. Conquering your enemies, enjoy a flourishing kingdom. I Myself have already killed these earlier. Become merely the instrument [*nimittamātram*], O Savyasācin [Arjuna].

34 Droṇa and Bhīṣma and Jayadratha and Karṇa, and the other brave warriors too, have already been destroyed by Me. Kill them, do not be afraid. Fight – you shall conquer your foes in war.

Sañjaya said:

35 Having heard this speech of Keśava, Arjuna folded his hands, trembling, offered obeisance again, and bowing down in extreme fear, addressed Kṛṣṇa in a choked voice.

Arjuna said:

36 O Hṛṣīkeśa [Kṛṣṇa], the world is made glad and rejoices in singing Your glory; the Rākṣasas, in fright, flee in all directions, and the multitudes of perfected beings bow down to You; this is rightly so.

37 And how would they not worship You, O Noble Soul, who are even superior to Brahma, the original maker? O Being without End, God of gods, Home to the universe – You are immutable and mutable, and You are also the Imperishable which is beyond these.

38 You are the first of the Gods, the Fundamental Being, the Supreme Haven of the universe. You are the Knower and what is to be known, the supreme abode. And You have pervaded this universe, who are infinite in form.

39 You are Vāyu [the wind], Yama [the God of Death], Agni [Fire], Varuṇa [the Sea-God], Śaśānka [the moon] and Prajāpati [Brahma]

and also the great grandfather of all. I acknowledge Your glory a thousand times, and bow down before You yet once more.

40 I prostrate in front of You, behind You, and on every side, O All in All. You procreate without end, Your prowess is beyond measure, You infiltrate all and are therefore All in All.

41 And for whatever I may have uttered in rashness to You, through error or familiarity, considering You my friend, unmindful of this Your greatness, such as 'Hey, Kṛṣṇa!; Hey, Yādava!; Hey, Friend!',

42 And for any insult I may have offered You, in fun, during play, in bed, or while seated, or at meals, alone or in the presence of others, O Acyuta, the Immeasurable, I pray to You, forgive me.

43 You, the father of the movable and unmovable in this world, are worthy of worship, the teacher of all teachers. There is no one who is Your equal in the three spheres. Then how can there be anyone greater, O Immeasurable Being?

44 Therefore, bowing down and prostrating myself before You, who are praiseworthy and mighty, I pray for Your favour. As a father his son, a friend his friend, a lover the loved one, so should You, O God, forgive me.

45 Having seen what no one ever has, I am happy but my mind is agitated with fear. Show me Your other form, O God. Be pleased with me, O God of gods, Pervader of the Universe!

46 Crowned, with the mace and the disc in Your hand as before, that is how I wish to see You. Take on again Your four-armed shape, O thousand-armed One of universal form.

Śrī Bhagavān said:

47 Being pleased, exerting My power of yoga, I have shown you, O Arjuna, this form which is supreme, radiant, universal, without end, fundamental, which no one except you has seen before.

48 Neither through the Vedas nor by yajñas, silent meditation, charity, ceremonial rituals, or severe austerities can this form of Mine be seen in this world of men by any other except you, O highest among the Kuru brave [Arjuna].

49 Do not be afraid, or aghast, at seeing this fearsome form of Mine. Abandoning fear, in a happy frame of mind, see again that other form of Mine.

Sañjaya said:

50 Having said which, Vāsudeva again showed Arjuna His own form. The Noble Soul, assuming again His benign aspect, gave solace to the terrified Arjuna.

Arjuna said:

51 O Janārdana, beholding again Your benign human form, my mind is now composed and returned to its normal state.

Śrī Bhagavān said:

52 This form of Mine, which you have seen, is extremely difficult to see. Even the gods are perpetually keen on seeing this form.

53 Neither through the Vedas, nor through austerities, charities or yajñas can I be seen in the form in which you have just seen Me.

54 But through fixed devotion to Me, it is possible to know Me thus, O Arjuna, and seeing Me truly, to enter into Me, O Vanquisher of foes.

55 He who performs all actions for Me, who regards Me as their end, who is devoted to Me, unattached, with no animosity towards all things, such a one attains Me, O Pāṇḍava.

In the Upaniṣad of the *Bhagavadgītā*, the knowledge
of Brahman the Supreme, the science of yoga,
and the dialogue between Śrīkṛṣṇa and Arjuna,
THIS IS THE ELEVENTH CHAPTER ENTITLED
'The Yoga of the Revelation of the Cosmic Form'

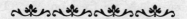

CHAPTER 12

The Yoga of Devotion

Arjuna said:

1 Those devotees who, always zealous in this way, worship You, or again the Immutable and Unmanifested, which among these are better knowers of yoga?

Śrī Bhagavān said:

2 Those who, focusing their thoughts on Me, always ardent, worship Me with the highest faith are, in My opinion, the best among the yogins.

3 But those who worship the Immutable, the Intangible, the Imperceptible, the All-Pervading, the Inconceivable, the Essential Unchanging Principle, the Immovable, the Permanent,

4 Having controlled their senses, possessed of equanimity in everything, concerned for the well-being of others, they also attain Me.

5 But the difficulty faced by those who focus their minds on the Imperceptible is greater, for the Imperceptible is perceived with difficulty by those with physical bodies.

6 But those who, their every action given to Me, focus on Me and worship Me, meditating on Me, with a single-minded devotion,

7 To them whose minds are fixed on Me, O Pārtha, I grant immediate deliverance from this ocean of mortality-bound worldly existence.

8 Focus your mind on Me only, let your intelligence dwell within Me. You shall dwell within Me hereafter, of this there can be no doubt.

9 But if such fixed and steady concentration on Me is not possible, then let Your aspiration persevere, through disciplined study, to attain Me, O Dhanañjaya.

10 If you find even such disciplined practice not possible, bear the sentiment of one to whom service of Me is the supreme goal. Even by performing all actions for Me, you shall attain success.

11 If even doing this is impossible for you, then take refuge in activity for Me alone and, with your mind controlled, surrender the fruit of all action.

12 For Knowledge is superior to Practice, Meditation to Knowledge, Surrendering the Fruit of Action to Meditation, and on such Surrender follows immediate peace.

13 He who bears no rancour towards anyone, is friendly and sympathetic, without egoism or self-pride, who is the same in pain and pleasure, forgiving,

14 The ever contented yogi, controlled, resolute, his mind and reason surrendered to Me, he, My devotee, is beloved of Me.

15 He from whom other men do not flinch and who does not flinch from others, and who is liberated from joy, anger, fear and excitement, is likewise beloved of Me.

16 He who expects nothing, is pure and works well, indifferent, composed, who has abandoned all purposed beginnings, he, My devotee, is beloved of Me.

17 He who feels neither joy nor hate, grief nor desire, who has given up good or evil, such a devotee is beloved of Me.

18 He who is the same towards enemies or friends, as well as towards honour or dishonour, cold and heat, happiness and unhappiness, and who is devoid of attachment,

19 Gives equal weight to censure and praise, is a man of few words, content with his lot, who is homeless [i.e. without a fixed goal], steady in mind, such a devotee is beloved of Me.

20 But those who with faith follow the nectar-like tenets stated above, regarding Me as the Supreme goal, those devotees are especially beloved of Me.

In the Upaniṣad of the *Bhagavadgītā*, the knowledge of Brahman the Supreme, the science of yoga, and the dialogue between Śrīkṛṣṇa and Arjuna,

THIS IS THE TWELFTH CHAPTER ENTITLED

'The Yoga of Devotion'

CHAPTER 13

The Yoga of the Division of the Cosmos into Body and Soul

Arjuna said:

Prakṛti, puruṣa, kṣetra, kṣetrajña, jñāna and jñeya – I would like to know these, Keśava.

Śrī Bhagavān said:

1 This very body, O Son of Kuntī, is called the *kṣetra* [field], and he who knows it is called the *kṣetrajña* [knower of the field] by those who understand these things.

2 Know that I am the *kṣetrajña* in all *kṣetras*, O Bhārata. I hold that knowledge of the field and of its knower is true knowledge.

3 What the field is, what its nature, its modifications, from what each evolved, who its knower is and what his powers, I shall explain briefly. Listen!

4 The ṛṣis have sung of this in many ways, in different metres, both of themselves and in the words of the Brahmasūtras, making the intent logical and perfectly conclusive.

5 The great [five gross] elements, conceit, reason, as well as the unmanifested, the ten senses and mind, and the five objects of the five senses,

6 Desire, hate, happiness, pain, the collective [organism], vitality and resolve – this briefly is the composite field [body] with its modifications.

7 Humility, the absence of hypocrisy, non-violence, tolerance, righteousness, service of the teacher, purity, constancy, control of the mind,

8 Indifference to the objects of the senses, negation of the self, awareness of birth, death, old age, ill-health and pain as evils,

9 Non-attachment, not holding on to one's son, wife, household and such things, a constant equanimity amid all desired and undesired occurrences,

10 Unswerving, concentrated, disciplined devotion to Me, having recourse to solitary places, an aversion to places where ordinary people meet,

11 Permanence in knowledge of the Spirit, a vision of the true essence of Divine Knowledge – all this is said to be knowledge, all else is ignorance.

12 I will tell you what is to be known, by knowing which one attains deliverance. It is the Supreme Brahman, without beginning, said to be neither imperishable nor perishable,

13 With hands and feet everywhere, eyes, heads and mouths on all sides, ears everywhere, He pervades everything, abiding in it.

14 He gives the impression of having the qualities of all the senses, yet is without the senses. Though unattached, He still supports everything. Void of qualities, He enjoys them nevertheless.

15 He is outside and within all things. He is immovable and yet movable. Subtle, He is incapable of being known. Far away, He is still near.

16 Undivided, He is still broken up among all things. He must be realised as one who, supporting all things, destroys them and refashions them again.

17 He is said to be the Radiance among radiances, beyond darkness, Knowledge, the object of knowledge, and that which can be known only through knowledge. He is seated in the hearts of everyone.

18 I have thus briefly explained the field, knowledge, and the object. My devotee, knowing this, is merged into My being.

19 Know that *prakṛti* and *puruṣa* are both without beginning. Know also that all forms and constituents arise from *prakṛti*.

20 Prakṛti [nature] is said to be the cause behind the act, its instrument and its doer, while puruṣa [soul] is said to be the cause behind the experience of pleasure and pain.

21 When puruṣa is positioned in prakṛti, it enjoys the constituents born of prakṛti. This marriage with the constituents is instrumental in its taking birth in good and bad wombs.

22 This Being who, close to prakṛti, witnesses its constituents, consents to them, adds to them, and experiences them, is termed the Great Lord, the Supreme Soul, the Supreme Puruṣa which dwells in the body.

23 He who in this way knows puruṣa and prakṛti, along with the constituents, in whatever way he acts, does not have rebirth.

24 Through meditation some see the Self within their selves by themselves, others through the Sāṁkhya Yoga [abandonment of action after the achievement of knowledge], and still others through the Karma Yoga.

25 Still others, unaware of these, worship on the basis of what they hear. And these also cross over beyond death, through their faith in what they have heard.

26 Whatever is born, movable or immovable, comes into being through the union of the kṣetra and the kṣetrajña – bear this in mind, O best of the Bhāratas.

27 He who sees the Supreme Lord, who is present equally in all creatures, who is not destroyed even when they are, he may be said to have truly perceived.

28 Perceiving the Lord as equally pervading everywhere, he does not let his self-sense destroy his true Self and, in that way, he attains a state of excellence.

29 He who perceives that all aspects of actions are performed only through prakṛti and also that the self is a non-doer, he may be said to have truly perceived.

30 On perceiving that the multifarious aspect of things is located in one point, from where it extends severally, he attains the Brahman.

31 Without beginning, devoid of qualities, the Supreme Self, imperishable, though stationed in the body, neither acts nor is touched in any way, O Son of Kuntī.

32 Just as ether, pervading everything, is unsmeared on account of its rarefied nature, in the same way the Self, present in everybody, is not besmirched.

33 Just as the Sun, alone, lights up this entire world, so also does the Keeper of the field light up this entire field, O Bhārata.

34 Those who in this way, through the eye of wisdom, perceive the difference between the field and the one who knows it, and the manner of release of all beings from prakṛti, they obtain the Supreme.

In the Upaniṣad of the *Bhagavadgītā*, the knowledge
of Brahman the Supreme, the science of yoga,
and the dialogue between Śrīkṛṣṇa and Arjuna,
THIS IS THE THIRTEENTH CHAPTER ENTITLED
'The Yoga of the Division of the Cosmos into Body and Soul'

CHAPTER 14

The Separation of the Three Guṇas

Śrī Bhagavān said:

1 Once again I shall tell you the supreme knowledge, the best of all knowledge, knowing which all sages have got to the highest state from this world.

2 Those who, taking refuge in this knowledge, are one with Me, are not reborn at the time of creation, nor do they die when this cosmos is dissolved.

3 The Great Brahma [prakṛti] is My womb, O Bhārata. In it I place My embryo, and from it all living creatures take birth.

4 Whatever beings take form in all the wombs, O Son of Kuntī, their womb is the great Brahma and I am the father who implants the seed.

5 O Mighty-armed, sattva, rajas and tamas, the guṇas born of prakṛti, keep bound in the body the unchangeable being which resides in the body.

6 Among these, the sattva constituent, pure as it is, gives light and health, O sinless one, and holds creatures in bondage through the attachment to happiness and to knowledge.

7 The rajas constituent tends to absorb one, and desire and attachment are born of it. O Son of Kuntī, it keeps creatures in bondage through attachment to action.

8 But tamas arises out of ignorance, and deceives all creatures, O Bhārata, keeping them in the bondage of neglect of duty, sloth and sleep.

9 Sattva makes one attached to happiness, rajas to action, O Bhārata, but tamas, enshrouding knowledge, attaches one to the neglect of duty.

10 O Bhārata, overcoming rajas and tamas, sattva predominates; rajas predominates in the same way over sattva and tamas, and tamas over sattva and rajas.

11 When through all the openings of the body the light of knowledge shines forth, it may be realised that the sattva constituent has increased.

12 Avarice, the urge for action, the taking on of action, discontent and desire – these are born, O best of the Bhāratas, when the rajas constituent has increased.

13 Darkness, a disinclination to act, neglect of duty, and confusion – these are born, O Descendant of the Kurus, when the tamas constituent has increased.

14 If the sattva predominates when a being dies, it goes to the pure spheres of those who know the Highest principles.

15 If the rajas predominates when it dies, it is reborn among those attached to action, and if it dies when the tamas predominates, it takes birth in the wombs of the ignorant species.

16 The fruit of virtuous action is said to be sāttvika, pure, but the fruit of action born of rajas is pain, and of tamas ignorance.

17 From sattva comes forth knowledge, avarice from rajas, and neglect of duty, delusion, and even ignorance from tamas.

18 Those who are sāttvika attain the higher spheres, the rājasa remain in the middle, while the tāmasa, immersed in baser qualities and tendencies, descend to the lower spheres.

19 When the visionary perceives that there is no agent besides the constituents, as also what is beyond them, he attains My form.

20 The embodied being, transcending these three constituents, causes of the body's birth, is liberated from birth, death, old age and pain, and attains immortality.

Arjuna said:

21 By what means is a man who has transcended the three constituents

to be distinguished, O Lord? What is his mode of living? How does he get past the three constituents?

Śrī Bhagavān said:

22 O Pāṇḍava, that man who does not feel an aversion towards enlightenment, advancement and delusion when they come upon him, nor craves for them when he does not have them,

23 Who is positioned like one indifferent, undisturbed by the constituents, who is steady and unmoved, aware that the constituents are merely acting their part,

24 Who views pain and pleasure alike, who is focused in his place, who sees a lump of earth, a stone and a piece of gold as the same, who weighs alike what is dear and what is disliked, constant, to whom disparagement and praise carry equal weight,

25 Who holds honour and dishonour alike, to whom a friend's or an enemy's side are the same, who has relinquished all initiative for action – such a man is regarded as having transcended the three constituents.

26 And he who single-mindedly serves Me with the yoga of devotion, transcends the three constituents and becomes capable of being merged in the Brahman.

27 Because I am the final seat of Brahman, the Immortal and Inexhaustible, of Eternal Dharma and of the Highest form of Bliss.

In the Upaniṣad of the *Bhagavadgītā*, the knowledge
of Brahman the Supreme, the science of yoga,
and the dialogue between Śrīkṛṣṇa and Arjuna,
THIS IS THE FOURTEENTH CHAPTER ENTITLED
'The Yoga of the Division of the Three Guṇas'

CHAPTER 15

The Yoga of the Supreme Self

Śrī Bhagavān said:

1 The imperishable aśvattha [peepal] is described as having its root above and branches below, with the Vedas for its leaves – and the one who has understood it thus has understood the Vedas.

2 Its branches, nourished by the constituents, spread out downwards and upwards, with shoots made of the objects of sense, while its roots, in the shape of action, stretch deep down into the world of men.

3 But here one cannot perceive its real form, nor its end, beginning or base. Cutting this incalculably deep-rooted aśvattha with a strong sword shaped of non-attachment,

4 One must then with these words go in quest of that seat from where, having reached it, no one returns: 'I go only to that Fundamental Principle [puruṣa] from whom this ancient cosmic process [pravṛtti] came forth.'

5 Those who are free from pride and ignorance, who have overcome the taint of attachment, who are firmly absorbed in the contemplation of the Spirit, free from all desire, from the contraries of pleasure and pain and such other delusions, attain this everlasting seat.

6 Neither does the sun illumine it, nor the moon or the fire. That is My supreme dwelling-place from where, having reached it, no one returns.

7 A minute particle of My fundamental being, taking on the form of a living soul in this living world, draws to itself the six, including the mind [the five senses and the mind], which abide in nature [prakṛti].

8 When the Lord assumes a body and when He leaves it, He takes them [the senses and mind] away just as the wind wafts away the fragrance from its spot.

9 Settling in the ears, eyes, the sense of touch, of taste and of smell, He enjoys the objects of the senses.

10 Those who are deluded do not see Him leaving the body or remaining in it, making experiences through contact with the constituents. But those who have the eye of knowledge see.

11 The yogins who strive see Him as installed within themselves, but those whose souls are not fully developed do not see Him even though they strive.

12 That radiance of the sun which lights up the entire world, and which is in the moon and fire, that radiance know to be Mine.

13 Likewise, entering the earth, I sustain all creatures by radiant energy. Becoming the sap-soaked soma [moon], I nurture all the world of plants.

14 Becoming the digestive fire, I live in the bodies of living creatures, and uniting with the prāṇa and apāna breaths I digest the four kinds of food [i.e. that which is eaten, sucked, licked or drunk].

15 Likewise am I fixed in every heart, and memory, knowledge and also their loss all come from Me. I am also He who is to be known by means of all the Vedas. I am the author of the Vedānta and also the knower of the Vedas.

16 There are two puruṣas in this sphere, *kṣara* and *akṣara*. *Kṣara* is all that is perishable, *akṣara* the imperishable which is at the root of all things.

17 But that most excellent of beings is other from these. It is called the Supreme Self, the Lord without End who pervades the three spheres and sustains them.

18 Since I go beyond the perishable and am a Being even more superior to the imperishable, therefore in ordinary speech as well as in the Vedānta am I regarded as the Supreme Being.

19 He who thus perceives, without being steeped in ignorance, Me as the Supreme Being, becomes one who knows all, and worships Me unreservedly with his whole self, O Bhārata.

20 O Flawless one, I have thus revealed this most secret among sastras. Knowledge of this will make a man wise, one who has performed all he needs to do, O Bhārata.

In the Upaniṣad of the *Bhagavadgītā*, the knowledge
of Brahman the Supreme, the science of yoga,
and the dialogue between Śrīkṛṣṇa and Arjuna,
THIS IS THE FIFTEENTH CHAPTER ENTITLED
'The Yoga of the Supreme Self'

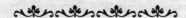

CHAPTER 16

The Divine and the Demoniacal Attributes

Śrī Bhagavān said:

1 Fearlessness, purity and sweetness in temperament, the judicious apportionment of knowledge and discipline, charity, endurance, sacrifice, study of the Vedas, austerity and integrity,

2 Non-violence, truthfulness, absence of anger, renunciation, tranquillity, overcoming narrow-mindedness, pity for all living creatures, freedom from greed, mildness, a sense of shame, steadiness,

3 Splendour, mercy, firmness, purity, absence of hatred or excessive self-esteem – these, O Bhārata, are the attributes of those who are born with a divine nature.

4 Deceit, arrogance, excessive self-esteem, anger, as also cruelty and ignorance, O Pārtha, are the attributes of those who are born with a demoniacal nature.

5 It is held that the divine attributes procure release, the demoniac bondage. Do not lament, O Pāṇḍava, you are born with the divine attributes.

6 Two types of creatures come into existence in this world: the divine and the demoniacal. I have elaborated upon the divine at length, now hear Me describe the demoniacal, O Pārtha.

7 Neither engagement in worldly action nor withdrawal from it is understood by the demoniacal. Neither purity, nor good behaviour or truth is present in them.

8 They say that the entire world is unreal, without foundation, without a Supreme Lord, created without a causal link – in short, that sensual enjoyment is its only *raison d'être*.

9 Adhering to this view, these soul-less people, vile, of feeble perception and cruel actions, spring into existence only to destroy the world.

10 Taking refuge in insatiable sensual desire, imbued with hypocrisy, self-esteem and arrogance, deluded into the wrong conclusions, they act with impure intentions.

11 Preoccupied with immeasurable concerns that cease only with death, firmly convinced that sensual enjoyment is everything, the ultimate end,

12 Bound by several hundred bonds of expectation, submitting to desire and anger, they aspire unjustly to accumulate huge amounts of wealth to indulge their cravings.

13 'I have obtained this today . . . I shall gratify this desire . . . This wealth I have acquired . . . and shall again . . .

14 'I have killed this foe . . . and I shall also slay others . . . I am sovereign, enjoyment is mine . . . I am prosperous, mighty and happy.

15 'I am rich and well born. Who is there who is like me? I shall enact sacrifices, dispense charity, enjoy myself' – in this way, misled through ignorance,

16 Misled by all kinds of thoughts, enmeshed in the net of mental confusion, immersed in sensual enjoyment, they fall into a filthy hell.

17 Conceited, unyielding, full of the pride and presumptuousness of wealth, they make a show of performing sacrifices in name only, ignoring the rules laid down in this regard.

18 Swollen with arrogance, power, pride, covetousness and anger, these slanderers loathe Me who am in their bodies and those of others.

19 Barbarous haters, the worst among men, evildoers are constantly flung by Me into demoniacal wombs in this worldly life.

20 Thus fallen into demoniacal wombs, these misguided ones go from birth to birth without reaching Me, O Son of Kuntī, finally reaching the lowest of low conditions.

21 The doorway to this hell is made of three folds, desire, anger and covetousness, and it leads to the destruction of the Self. Therefore, one should abandon these three.

22 O Son of Kuntī, he who is delivered from these three entrances to darkness does what benefits his Self, and thereby reaches the highest state.

23 But he who has abandoned the code of the *śāstras* [sciences, here essentially dealing with prescribed codes of conduct], doing what he desires, does not attain either perfection or happiness or the highest state.

24 Therefore, accepting the authority of the *śāstras* as regards what ought or ought not to be done, and knowing what the code of the *śāstras* says, you should act accordingly in this world.

In the Upaniṣad of the *Bhagavadgītā*, the knowledge
of Brahman the Supreme, the science of yoga,
and the dialogue between Śrīkṛṣṇa and Arjuna,
THIS IS THE SIXTEENTH CHAPTER ENTITLED
'The Divine and the Demoniacal Attributes'

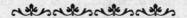

CHAPTER 17

The Yoga of the Threefold Division of Faith

Arjuna said:

1 Those who do not observe the śāstric codes but perform sacrifices in full faith – what of their state, O Kṛṣṇa? Is it that of sāttvika, rājasa, or tāmasa?

Śrī Bhagavān said:

2 The faith of embodied beings is of three kinds, consequent upon their temperament – sāttvika, rājasa and tāmasa. Hear about it.

3 Every man's faith takes the form of his essential nature, Bhārata. Man is composed of his faith – as his faith, so is he formed.

4 The sāttvika sacrifice to the gods, the rājasa to the minor gods and the demons, while the remaining, the tāmasa, sacrifice to corpses and ghosts.

5 Fierce austerities contrary to the *śāstras* are performed by those who, filled with sanctimoniousness and conceit, driven by the force of desire and passion,

6 Being foolish, oppress the five fundamental elements in their body as also Me, who fill that body. Know that these are demoniacal in temperament.

7 The food beloved of every creature is also of three kinds, as are sacrifices, austerities and gifts. Listen to me explain the distinctions.

8 Foods enhancing life, sap, strength, health, happiness and love, which are sweet, greasy and stay in the body are beloved of the sāttvika.

9 Sharp, sour, salty, heating, spicy, harsh, burning foods which produce pain, sorrow and disease are liked by the rājasa.

10 Food which has remained for some time, its flavour gone, foul-smelling, stale, defiled by tasting, and impure is dear to the tāmasa.

11 That sacrifice offered without any desire for the fruit, in accordance with the prescribed rites, with a composed mind, whose performance is seen as a duty, is sāttvika.

12 But the one performed with a desire for reward or for mere ostentation, know such a sacrifice, O best of the Bhāratas, to be a rājasa one.

13 And that performed in disregard of the *śāstras*, without the distribution of food, recitation of mantras, or conferring of gifts on Brahmins is termed a tāmasa sacrifice.

14 Worship of the gods, the twice-born, the gurus and the learned; keeping clean, integrity, celibacy and non-violence – these are described as bodily penance.

15 Speaking that which does not offend, which is true, welcome and beneficial, as well as habitual reading aloud of the Vedas are termed the penance of speech.

16 Tranquillity, gentleness, silence, self-control and purity of feelings are called mental penance.

17 These three forms of penance, observed with absolute faith and with no desire for reward, with a mind in total control, are described as sāttvika.

18 Those penances performed with a view to obtaining respect, esteem and reverence, or in a hypocritical way, are rājasa, and are transient and unstable.

19 Those penances performed out of purposeless obduracy, through self-torture or with the intention of hurting others, are described as tāmasa.

20 That gift which is conferred on one who has not obliged the giver, in the belief that it is one's duty to give, and which is given after duly assessing the place, time and the person, is regarded as sāttvika.

21 But a gift conferred in return for some favour, or an expectation of some future reward, or when one grudges the giving, is regarded as rājasa .

22 And a gift made at an inappropriate place or moment, or to one not worthy of it, without due regard or in a disrespectful way is termed tāmasa.

23 'Aum-Tat-Sat' – this is the three-fold definition of the Brahman, in accordance with which the Brahmins, the Vedas and the sacrifices came into being in former times.

24 Thence, uttering the word 'Aum', the exponents of Brahman always begin all rites of sacrifice, charity and penance laid down in the scriptures.

25 Uttering the word 'Tat', those who seek release perform the rites of sacrifice and penance and the varied acts of charity, without looking to the reward.

26 Reality and saintliness are what the word 'Sat' conveys. Likewise, the word 'Sat' is applied to commendable acts, O Pārtha.

27 Being resolute in sacrifice, penance and charity is also called 'Sat', and any action performed to that end is likewise known as 'Sat'.

28 Any sacrifice into the fire, any giving, any penance, or any rite, which is enacted without faith, is called 'asat', O Pārtha, of no benefit either in the after-life or in this one.

In the Upaniṣad of the *Bhagavadgītā*, the knowledge
of Brahman the Supreme, the science of yoga,
and the dialogue between Śrīkṛṣṇa and Arjuna,
THIS IS THE SEVENTEENTH CHAPTER ENTITLED
'The Yoga of the Threefold Division of Faith'

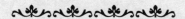

CHAPTER 18

The Yoga of Deliverance Through Renunciation

Arjuna said:

1 O Mighty-armed, O Hṛṣīkeśa, I wish to know in individual wise the essential nature of renunciation [*saṁnyāsa*] as well as of abandonment [*tyāga*], O Keśiniṣūdana [Kṛṣṇa].

Śrī Bhagavān said:

2 The wise see Sāṁnyāsa as a giving up of acts inspired by desire. The abandonment of the fruit of all actions, say the learned, is tyāga.

3 Some learned men say that action, being flawed, should be given up, others that sacrifice, charity, penance and action should not be abandoned.

4 Hear from Me therefore, O best of the Bhāratas, what is certain about tyāga. O best among men, tyāga is regarded as being three-fold.

5 Sacrifice, charity, penance and action should never be abandoned. They must be performed, for sacrifice, charity, penance and action cleanse even the wise.

6 Hence, even these acts should be performed, detachedly and abandoning the fruit. O Pārtha, this is My certain and ultimate opinion.

7 Any action prescribed by one's dharma should not be renounced. Abandoning it because of ignorance is described as tāmasa.

8 If pain or the fear of bodily suffering results in the abandonment of action, he who abandons it is rājasa, and will not gain the fruit of tyāga.

9 When a prescribed action is performed as a duty, O Arjuna, having given up attachment as well as the fruit, such abandonment is held to be a sāttvika one.

10 He who abandons and is neither averse to action which does not benefit him nor attached to action which promotes welfare, has the sāttvika temperament, and is wise and liberated from doubt.

11 Nor is it at all possible for any embodied being totally to abandon action. Hence, only he who abandons the fruit of action is said to be a tyāgin.

12 Imperfect, perfect, and a mixture of both constitute the three kinds of fruit of action which the one who has not renounced obtains after death; the man who renounces gets nothing at all.

13 I shall tell you, O Mighty-armed, the five essential causes specified in the Sāṁkhya philosophy as regulating all actions.

14 The seat of action as well as the doer, the various kinds of implements, the several forms of effort, and the fifth of these, which is the divine agency.

15 Whatever action a man may begin by means of his body, speech or mind, whether it be justified or unjustified, these are its five causes.

16 When this is how things are, he who through folly or unpractised reasoning perceives himself alone as the doer does not perceive at all.

17 He who does not possess the conviction that he is the doer, and whose reasoning is untainted, though slaying other persons cannot be said to have slain them nor does this bind him.

18 Knowledge, the knowable and the knower form the three-fold impulse to action. The implement, the action and the doer form the three-fold basis of action.

19 That knowledge, action and the doer are of three kinds, in accordance with the difference in the three constituents, is enunciated in the Sāṁkhya system which deals with the constituents. Listen to what has been said of them.

20 That knowledge which sees one inexhaustible principle in all created beings, the undivided in all that is divided, is called sāttvika knowledge.

21 Knowledge which perceives diverse principles in different created things on account of their being separate is known as rājasa knowledge.

22 But that trifling knowledge which is unreasonably restricted to what has been done, seeing it as all-encompassing, with no concern for its cause and no understanding of its fundamentals, is called tāmasa knowledge.

23 An action which is prescribed, which is performed without attachment, without love or hatred, is termed sāttvika.

24 But that action which is performed laboriously, by him who desires gratification or is motivated by self-esteem, is termed rājasa.

25 That action which is begun through ignorance, with no thought for consequences, disadvantage, harm, or whether one has the human capacity for it, is termed tāmasa.

26 He who is free from attachment, whose speech is devoid of egoism, who is endowed with fortitude and enthusiasm, and unaffected by success or failure, is termed a sāttvika doer.

27 He who is attached to the objects of the senses, who is keen on the fruit of action, covetous, harmful by nature, impure and swayed by joy and sorrow is termed a rājasa doer.

28 He who is of unsteady mind, unrefined, obdurate, a cheat, who deprives people of their goods, is indolent, dejected, and who procrastinates, is termed a tāmasa doer.

29 Listen to the three-fold division of reason as well as of steadiness, arising out of the three constituents, which I am setting forth separately in their entirety, O Dhanañjaya.

30 That reason which perceives when an action is begun or not begun, what ought to be done or what ought not to be done, what should be feared or what should not be feared, what leads to bondage and what releases, O Pārtha, is called sāttvika.

31 That reason by which one cannot properly discriminate between the righteous and the unrighteous, between what ought to be done and what ought not to be done, O Pārtha, is called rājasa.

32 That reason which sees as righteous what is unrighteous, being shrouded in darkness, and produces a distorted view of everything, is called tāmasa.

33 That unswerving steadfastness by which, through yoga, one conducts the activities of the mind, life-breaths and the senses, O Pārtha, is sāttvika.

34 That steadfastness by which one maintains duty, desire and riches, in hope of the fruit when the occasion arises, is rājasa.

35 That steadfastness by which he who is feeble-minded does not abandon sleep, fear, grief, dejection and pride, O Pārtha, is tāmasa.

36 Now hear from Me the three kinds of happiness, O best of the Bhāratas. That absorption to which a man journeys through long practice, and wherein unhappiness comes to an end.

37 That which is like poison at the start and like nectar in its effects, that happiness is said to be sāttvika, and arises from the serenity of self-understanding.

38 That which arises from the contact of the senses with their objects, which is like nectar to start with but poisonous in its effects, that happiness is said to be rājasa.

39 That happiness which deludes the soul both at the start and in its effects, which arises from sleep, laziness and neglect of one's duties, is said to be tāmasa.

40 There is no being either on earth or even among the gods in the firmament who is free from these three constituents of nature.

41 O Vanquisher of foes, the duties of Brahmins, Kṣatriyas, Vaiśyas and Śūdras are distinctively prescribed in keeping with the qualities inherent in their natures.

42 Peace, self-control, austerities, cleanliness, patience, integrity, spiritual wisdom, empirical knowledge and faith in a future world are the duties of a Brahmin, arising from his nature.

43 Valour, prowess, fortitude, resolve, not fleeing from battle, generosity and a lordly disposition are the duties of a Kṣatriya, arising from his nature.

44 Agriculture, rearing cattle and trade are the duties of a Vaiśya, arising from his nature; the work of a servant is the duty of a Śūdra, arising from his nature.

45 By being absorbed in performing his own duty, man attains perfection. Listen to how he who sticks to his own duty attains perfection.

46 He from whom all created things arise and who has pervaded this whole – by the worship of Him through the performance of his own duty does a man attain perfection.

47 Action according to one's own dharma, though flawed, is better than another dharma, though easy to execute. In performing one's naturally ordained duty, a man does not incur sin.

48 That action which is inherent in one's nature, O Son of Kuntī, should not be given up, even if flawed, because all enterprises are shrouded in faults as fire in smoke.

49 A man whose mind is unattached to anything, whose mind is subdued, and from whom all desire is departed, by means of renunciation reaches the supreme state beyond all action.

50 O Son of Kuntī, I shall explain to you in short how, attaining perfection, he attains the Brahman, the supreme state of wisdom.

51 He who, possessed with a pure understanding, firmly disciplining himself, giving up sound and other sense-impressions, avoids love or aversion,

52 Lives in a solitary place, eats little, his body, speech and mind under control, always absorbed in meditation, renouncing all passion,

53 Giving up self-conceit, force, pride, desire, anger, possessions, becoming selfless and of serene mind – he is worthy to be merged with Brahman.

54 Merged in the Brahman, at peace with himself, he neither laments nor desires anything. Seeing all things as the same, he acquires supreme devotion towards Me.

55 By means of devotion he gets knowledge of My particulars, what I amount to, and who I really am. Then, when he knows the essential Me, he enters Me.

56 While ever performing all actions taking shelter in Me, by My favour he attains an everlasting and imperishable position.

57 Having mentally dedicated all actions to Me, looking upon Me as the Supreme, taking refuge in the yoga of understanding, keep your thoughts always focused on Me.

58 Focusing your thoughts on Me, you shall by My favour overcome all difficulties. But if you pay no heed because of self-conceit, you shall be as nothing.

59 If, resorting to self-conceit, you maintain 'I will not fight', your conviction regarding this is baseless: nature will compel you to do it.

60 Being bound by the action arising out of your nature, O Son of Kuntī, you will have to do that which, contrary to your nature and through delusion you do not wish to do.

61 The Lord dwells in the hearts of all beings, Arjuna, and by His divine illusion makes all creatures whirl as if placed in a machine.

62 Go unto Him for shelter with all your heart, O Bhārata. By His grace you shall attain supreme peace and an everlasting home.

63 In this way have I revealed to you this knowledge, a mystery among mysteries. Contemplate on it fully, and do whatever you wish to.

64 Listen once more to My ultimate statement, the mystery of all mysteries. You being dearly beloved of Me, I shall tell you that which shall benefit you.

65 Focus your mind on Me; be My devotee; perform sacrifices to Me; prostrate before Me – in this way you shall come to Me, I assure you of this truth because you are dear to Me.

66 Giving up all other dharmas, come to Me alone for shelter. I shall release you from all sins, have no more fear.

67 Never should you speak about this to anyone who does not observe austerities, who has no devotion, who does not listen to what is said, or who speaks ill of Me.

68 He who interprets this supreme mystery to My devotees, displaying the highest devotion to Me, will come and reach Me without a doubt.

69 Nor will there be among all men anyone whose service is dearer to Me than his, or any man in this universe who will be more beloved of Me than he is.

70 I shall consider whoever studies this conversation on dharma between us both as having worshipped Me by performing a Sacrifice of Knowledge.

71 That man who listens to it with faith and without derision, he too shall be liberated and acquire the happy realms of those who have been righteous in action.

72 O Pārtha, have you heard all this with a focused mind? Has your bewilderment, linked to ignorance, been thoroughly destroyed, Dhanañjaya?

Arjuna said:

73 My ignorance has been destroyed and I have got back my memory through Your grace, O Acyuta. I shall be steady, freed of doubt. I shall do what You have stated.

Sañjaya said:

74 And so have I heard this marvellous dialogue between Vāsudeva and the noble-souled Pārtha, which made my hair stand on end.

75 By the grace of Vyāsa, I heard this mystery of mysteries, the yoga expounded by Kṛṣṇa, Himself the Lord of Yoga, in person.

76 O sovereign, recalling over and over again this marvellous and holy dialogue between Keśava and Arjuna, I quiver repeatedly with joy.

77 O king, as I recall over and over again that most marvellous form of Hari [Kṛṣṇa], my sense of wonder is great and I rejoice again and again.

78 Wherever there is the Lord of Yoga, Kṛṣṇa, and wherever there is Pārtha the archer, there I hold that there is bound to be wealth, victory, everlasting prosperity and morality.

In the Upaniṣad of the *Bhagavadgītā*, the knowledge
of Brahman the Supreme, the science of yoga,
and the dialogue between Śrīkṛṣṇa and Arjuna,
THIS IS THE EIGHTEENTH CHAPTER ENTITLED
'The Yoga of Deliverance through Renunciation'

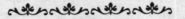